W9-DGF-955

Miss Frost
Ices the Imp

A Nocturne Falls Mystery

Jayne Frost, book two

KRISTEN PAINTER

MISS FROST ICES THE IMP

A Nocturne Falls Mystery
Jayne Frost, Book Two

Copyright © 2016 Kristen Painter

All rights reserved. No part of this book may be reproduced in any form or by any electronic or mechanical means, including information storage and retrieval systems—except in the case of brief quotations embodied in critical articles or reviews—without permission in writing from the author.

This book is a work of fiction. The characters, events, and places portrayed in this book are products of the author's imagination and are either fictitious or are used fictitiously. Any similarity to real person, living or dead, is purely coincidental and not intended by the author.

ISBN: 978-1-941695-20-3

Published in the United States of America.

Welcome to Nocturne Falls—the town that celebrates Halloween 365 days a year.

Jayne Frost is a lot of things. Winter elf, Jack Frost's daughter, Santa Claus's niece, heir to the Winter Throne and now...private investigator. Sort of.

When she buys a sealed box at an estate sale and cat-related circumstances cause that box to be opened, life in Nocturne Falls starts to go haywire. Jayne has no choice but to figure out what she unleashed and how to recapture it.

But Jayne suspects the woman behind the box is hiding something. Something that could cause a town resident serious trouble. Or worse, to lose their life.

With the help of her two favorite guys, a sexy vampire and a hot summer elf, and a few new friends, Jayne tackles what feels like an impossible mission. And winds up almost iced herself.

I sucked in a giddy breath as my gaze landed on the tackiest, most wonderful thing I'd ever seen. Maybe it was the unholy hour of seven A.M. making me delirious, but I grabbed the little framed velvet Elvis painting and held on to it for dear life, instantly sure everyone else at the estate sale was coveting my incredible find.

And why wouldn't they be? It wasn't just any Elvis painting. It was Elvis as a *cat* in the white Vegas jumpsuit complete with real hot-glued rhinestones, plastic gems and big Puss In Boots eyes. It was glorious.

"You can't be serious. Are you buying that?" Juniper joined me, a couple treasures of her own in her arms. "It's a bedazzled nightmare."

"Agreed, which is what makes it impossible to look away from. I love it." Just because my father is Jack Frost and I'm the Winter Princess doesn't

1

mean I only like designer stuff and fine art. *Hardly*. I held it up so the sun caught the adornments and sent them into fits of sparkle. "I'm going to hang it over Spider's feeding station. I think he'll find it very aspirational."

Juniper's brows lifted. "You think it's going to make your cat want to be an Elvis impersonator?"

"There are worse paths he could take." I shrugged. "And he already thinks he's the king of the apartment."

She grinned. "True. Find anything else you can't live without?"

I lifted my basket to show her the rest of my treasures. "I found a cool decorative box. The lid is locked, and possibly also glued into place. I can't get it open, but I can work on that when I get it home. Either way, it's pretty. And if I get it open, I can stash candy in it."

She picked the box up. "Cool. It's very pretty. Do you think there's anything in it?"

"I doubt it. Doesn't have much weight to it and there's nothing rattling around inside that I could hear."

She gave it a shake and a listen. "Yeah, probably empty. Still sort of exciting. Might be an old love letter or something in there that doesn't make noise."

"I'll be sure to tell you if I discover anything."

She put the box back and took out the hula

dancer salt and pepper shakers I'd found, giving them a skeptical glance. "I must admit, you have very different tastes than I expected. They're cute in their own way, but just not what I thought you'd go for."

"I thought they were fun. Plus, I think tropical might be my theme."

Juniper returned them to the basket. "You're a winter elf and you want to decorate your apartment to look like the islands?"

"You're a winter elf, too. Don't you think it would be a nice change from Christmas all the time?" Although, unlike Juniper, I'd spent most of my life in the North Pole. And Santa was my uncle on my mother's side. Was it any wonder I was starting to have tropical fantasies?

"I see your point." She glanced around at the tables of items on display. "Quite a collection of stuff, huh? The people who owned this house had some pretty eclectic tastes, but then, the rich are weird." She bit her lip. "Present company excluded."

"I'm only rich adjacent." My parents had the money. And sure, someday those funds would be mine when I took the throne, but for right now my best assets were my family name and the connections that gave me. Okay, my legs weren't bad either.

Juniper gave me a look as she returned the salt

and pepper shakers to the basket. "I thought you wanted things to decorate your apartment with, though. Bigger stuff."

"I do." That was the whole reason we'd come out so early to this estate sale. We had the addresses of two more yard sales to hit after this. But this was the biggie. One of the better houses in town, according to Juni. Who also insisted that arriving first thing was the only way to get the good stuff. So…that meant this was all be the good stuff, right? "I found a rug and a big painting, but they're still inside the house since they're obviously too large to fit in my basket. You want to go in and take a look at them?"

"Absolutely."

"Cool. First, show me what you found."

She held up a small evening bag covered in jet beads with a matching fringe along the bottom. "I don't have much use for a purse like this, but I collect these little antique bags, and I think they're so pretty. Plus, I don't have a black one. Kind of silly to collect something so impractical, but we all have our weaknesses."

"It's gorgeous. And you could definitely use it. Get Pete to take you to Café Claude." Pete and Juniper had been seeing each other pretty regularly since we'd all gone to the spaghetti dinner fundraiser at the fire station.

She nodded as she slipped the purse's chain

over her arm. "That's a good idea. We keep meaning to go there. I'm getting this, too." She lifted a small ceramic thing out of her shopping basket. It had a carved design on one side and a squatty handle on the other.

"What is that? A stamp?"

"It's a cookie press. Isn't it pretty?"

"It is. Does that mean you're going to be baking soon?"

She put it back in her basket. "I have been getting the itch."

"I'm happy to be your taste tester."

"I have no doubt." She took the purse off her arm and lay it in the basket too. "All right, show me this rug and painting."

We went into the house, a big old Victorian with just the slightest creepiness about it. A few other people were milling about, but the only things for sale inside were big. With prices to match.

I stopped at the entrance to the room off the foyer. Maybe a sitting room or something? I wasn't sure, and most of the furniture had been wrapped in blankets for moving, making it hard to tell. "This is the rug."

"It's gorgeous." Juniper nodded. "I love that Oriental style. Very classy. And the tan and green will look great on the hardwood in your apartment. Is it expensive?" Then she laughed. "Never mind. I know you can afford it."

"Only because my parents are helping me a little," I confessed. They'd dropped a tidy sum into my bank account as a housewarming gift. Had I mentioned that being the Winter Princess didn't mean I was filthy rich? My parents, on the other hand, were loaded. I could have asked for extra, but making my own way was more rewarding, and I had a salary now that I was manager of the Santa's Workshop Toy Store in Nocturne Falls.

"Very nice of them." Juniper looked around. "Is the painting you mentioned in here too?"

"No, it's in the next room." We walked a little farther into the study, and I showed her. "What do you think?"

"I think I can understand the hula dancers now." She crossed her arms and appeared to give the art some genuine consideration.

It was just a landscape, but staring at it made me feel like I could actually hear the waves, feel the sun on my face and taste the salt in the air. Juniper hadn't said anything more, so I felt the need to defend my choice. "I love it. I think it's like a vacation on a canvas."

A gentle grin curved Juniper's mouth, and her eyes stayed on the painting. "I think it's incredible. Wherever it is, I want to go there."

The woman running the sale approached us with a smile. "It's Hanalei Bay. Also known as Bali Hai. In Hawaii. Isn't it lovely? The owners picked it up on one of their many trips there. They collected things from all of their travels. I'm Bryn, by the way. I'm the agent handling the estate's liquidation. Are you interested in the painting?"

"Yes. And the tan rug in the front room." I lifted my basket. "And this stuff."

Juniper stepped forward. "What's your best price, since she's buying so much?"

Bryn smiled. "I'll sharpen my pencil and get right back to you." She started to walk away, then stopped and turned toward us again. "Just so you know, all sales are final, and you must be able to take these things with you today. Do you have a vehicle?"

"Um…" I glanced at Juniper. Winter elves weren't exactly weaklings, but we'd ridden the company-provided bikes here. I couldn't exactly balance the rug, the painting and my other purchases while pedaling. "I need to make a phone call. But it shouldn't be a problem."

"All right. I'll go work some magic on the total and be back in a few minutes."

As Bryn left us, I nudged Juni and gave her a thumbs-up. "Way to go on asking for a discount. I never would have thought of that."

"It's what these sales are all about. But don't change the subject."

"I wasn't—"

"Oh, really? And who are you going to call?"

"You know who." I sighed. "I don't have any choice if I want to get this stuff home. He's the only one I know with a truck."

"You could call an iRyde."

"After all the money I just spent, you want me to spend more?"

Juniper raised her brows. "You're going to owe him."

"Don't remind me." I pulled out my phone and dialed one of Nocturne Falls' hottest citizens, Cooper Sullivan. And I wasn't just making a pun because he was a fireman. And an incredibly good-looking one. He was a summer elf, the opposite of my kind. Heat and fire were the calling cards of summer elves, just like cold and ice belonged to us.

Cooper was also my ex-boyfriend from college. We'd broken up due to a shady third party (my former best friend Lark, who really ought to be known as She Who Shall Not Be Named) and her lies, but Coop and I had recently made up. Meaning we were friends again, but not really dating. Well, sort of dating. But not in a serious way.

It was hard to say exactly what Cooper and I were doing now. Casually dating maybe? We'd been totally into each other in college, but the years between then and now had been filled with a lot of bad feelings and unhappy memories. Moving past all that was further complicated by the fact that I'd come to Nocturne Falls in a magical disguise that hid who I really was. It was all part of my attempt to uncover why employees at the toy shop were going missing.

During that attempt and in that disguise, I dated Cooper. Just a few times. But, hey, I was on a fact-finding mission and Cooper was dialed into the town, being a fireman and all. It was just part of doing my job.

In the interest of full disclosure, I should mention that some of the dates had included kissing. Really good kissing.

I'd since come clean about who I was, having solved the missing-elves business, so Cooper knew the truth. We were doing our best to be friends now, though we hadn't seen much of each other the last few weeks. Mostly because I'd been avoiding him. I know. Not the nicest of me. But I was so torn about how to feel when it came to Cooper. I liked him. But we had some strange history. And we were different people now than we'd been in college. Who wasn't?

Juniper thought I should be friends with him but move on romantically. She liked Cooper as a friend, too, but after I told her what had happened between us in college, she was convinced that if he had really loved me then, he would have fought harder.

Not that she was so fond of the other man in my

life. Greyson Garrett. Dark, mysterious, handsome and a little dangerous, Greyson was everything my mother had ever warned me about in a man. And then some. He was also a vampire with the most delicious Irish accent. I could listen to him talk all day. But more on that tasty hunk of fanged goodness later.

Cooper answered on the fourth ring. "Jayne?"

"Yep, it's me."

"Hey, what have you been up to?"

"Work mostly. Getting the store back on track and bringing new employees in, getting them trained, all that stuff. It's been crazy busy." That wasn't a lie, but I'd had some time to hang out with Juniper and Buttercup, the other store employee I'd become friends with, so it wasn't as if I'd been working non-stop.

"I'm sure you've been swamped. How do you like being manager?"

"I love it, actually." It was the first job I'd had that felt right.

"Good." He paused, and I could sense him leaving the small talk behind. "Any room in your schedule for lunch?"

And there it was. "Oh, I always make time to eat. You know me." I made a face at Juniper, who made an I-told-you-so face right back at me.

He laughed. "I meant lunch with me."

I knew that. But I was all about avoidance.

Sadly, that wasn't going to get the rug and the painting and all this other paraphernalia back to my apartment. And if Cooper was willing to help, I'd make it worth his while. Because that was the right thing to do for a friend. "I'll tell you what, if you can do me a favor today, I'll fix you dinner tonight. At my place. I have some work to do when I get back, schedules to write up and inventories to run, that kind of stuff, but maybe around seven, you could come—"

"Done."

Okay, he was more eager to see me than I'd anticipated. "You don't know what the favor is. Or what I'm making for dinner." Spaghetti and meat sauce, because that was easy, yummy and the perfect excuse to have tiramisu for dessert.

"Whatever you make will be fine. What's the favor?" There was a smile in his voice. "Should I be worried?"

I hoped not. "I need help getting a rug and a painting from an estate sale back to my apartment."

"I see. You're just interested in me for my muscles."

He had no idea. Or maybe he did. I played it off. "If muscles is what you call your pickup truck, then you've figured me out."

He laughed. "Let me throw on some clothes, and I can be there in ten. So long as you aren't miles away. Where is this place?"

Throw on some clothes? What was he wearing now? Or not wearing? I reined my thoughts in. "Not far. We're over on Phantom Lane."

He whistled. "The ritzy part of town."

"Yeah, we're at a big Victorian that's having an estate sale. Nasty divorce is the scuttlebutt. Anyway, there's lots of cool stuff."

"I'll find it. Call you when I get there if I don't see you first." He hung up.

I tucked my phone into my purse. "He's on his way."

"And you're making him dinner? Sounds like a fun evening." Juniper's knowing wink wasn't helpful.

"I like him." I really did.

"I know. But you also like Greyson. Or are you throwing him aside? Which would be fine with me."

"I'm not throwing Greyson aside." I liked him, too.

"Then do you like Cooper enough to give him a second chance? Because that's probably what he thinks this is."

"Yeah, I don't know." Is that what I'd just done? Told Cooper I was ready to start something again? I couldn't very well back out now. And frankly, I wasn't sure if I wanted to. There was no rule that said I couldn't date two guys. We were living in liberated times. And I was the Winter Princess! I could date around if I wanted to. "This could be like a test to see how we do together now that he knows who I really am."

She nodded, then tipped her head. "Are you going to let him kiss you if he tries?"

"I'll only tell you that if you make those cookies." Really, I had no idea if this was going to be that kind of evening. Probably not. It kind of felt like Cooper and I were starting over, and I wasn't sure if that's the direction we should be headed in. Not when I was already having feelings for Greyson.

Although I had loved Cooper once. Thought I'd be married to him, actually. There was a time when I'd had my whole future planned out, and all of it included Cooper. Funny how things change. The thought made me a little melancholy.

Juniper poked me.

"What?"

She tipped her head. I looked in the direction she'd indicated.

Bryn walked up to us, bill in hand. She presented it to me. "How does this look?"

I took the paper. She'd given me an extra twenty percent off. "It looks great, thank you."

Bryn smiled. "Will that be cash or credit?"

"You take credit cards?"

"We do." She took out her phone and plugged a card reader into it. "Don't you love technology?"

By the time Cooper was due to arrive, I'd found

and paid for a few more things. A set of pillows for the couch, a fancy gargoyle robe hook, a picture for the bathroom and a waffle iron. Because who doesn't love waffles? Especially with ice cream and hot fudge. I also never turn down sprinkles. Which could be my life's motto.

Speaking of tasty things, Cooper was walking toward Juniper and me looking way too good for this early on a Saturday morning. I took a breath, realizing I'd forgotten just how perfect the man was. Or maybe I'd blocked it out.

The whole sun-kissed surfer vibe was sort of a summer elf trait, but Cooper took it to a different level and made it look effortless with that athletic gait of his and that perfectly tousled dirty-blond hair.

I suddenly wished I'd at least put lip gloss on. Instead, I was standing here in cut-off jean shorts, a Howler's tank top (free because I'd caught it while standing in the crowd of the Panic Parade in May) and some recently purchased rubber flip-flops. My real effort today had been hauling my carcass out from under the covers early enough to avoid the blizzard Juniper had threatened me with if I didn't wake up in time. She might not have been the most skilled of winter elves, but I was sure she wasn't kidding about the avalanche.

I never should have given her a key to my apartment.

The clothes Cooper had thrown on were a

ragged pair of khaki shorts and a faded T-shirt. Not much of an effort either, but on him it worked. Overtime. The clothes did nothing to hide his tall, muscular frame. His hair was, at best, finger-combed, and the sandy stubble covering his square jaw made my fingers itch to touch it. He pushed his sunglasses on top of his head as he joined us, his brilliant blue eyes crinkling at the corners with his smile. "Morning, ladies."

"Hi, Cooper. Nice of you to help," Juniper said while poking me in the back where Cooper couldn't see.

I was pretty sure she was commenting on his hotness. "Yeah, thanks, Cooper."

"You're welcome." He looked around. "Where's your stuff?"

"In the house. I'll show you."

Juniper grabbed my arm before I left. "We're obviously not hitting any of the other sales, so I'm going to head back. That way I can get my shower and get into the store without rushing. It is Saturday."

Saturdays were an event in the shop. Snowy Saturdays, we called them. It was the day we used our collective magic to make it snow in the store. The customers loved it and we were always busy. "No problem. I'll see you later. Thanks."

"You're welcome." She glanced at Cooper. "Have fun."

She bopped away before I could say anything more. I knew she needed to get ready for work, but I also knew she was leaving me alone with Cooper on purpose. My guess was that, as much as she thought Greyson was a bad idea, she probably thought Cooper wasn't, despite her opinion that he hadn't fought hard enough for me in college. Hey, she'd known him for nearly four years and considered him a friend. I couldn't blame her for siding with Team Cooper.

Greyson was relatively new in town and, as I mentioned, a vampire. That was the part she didn't like, the vampire bit. She just worried about all the unknowns that came with being one of the more dangerous supernaturals. But Greyson hadn't done anything to deserve the worry or speculation. He was a great guy and one I liked very much.

There was no way I was remotely ready to pick one guy over the other.

"Lead the way, Princess." Cooper winked at me.

I controlled my urge to roll my eyes. "Come on."

Cooper and I went into the house to retrieve my things. I found Bryn and told her we were taking my purchases. Better that than someone think we were just walking off with stuff. She gave us the go-ahead and my receipt, which I had walked off without getting earlier. Too discombobulated with thoughts of Cooper, apparently. I stuffed it in my pocket without a second glance.

I took Cooper into the dining room and showed him the rug. "Nice, huh?"

"Very." He bent down at one corner, looking at me expectantly.

I crouched down at the other one, and we rolled it up. The thing was heavy. This was more work than I'd expected. "Did I mention there would be dessert? Because this much work definitely merits dessert."

"I won't say no to that." His end was going faster, so he stopped to let me catch up and straighten things out. "You know what I like."

There was a loaded statement. And I had no comeback. Instead, I made a mental note to pick up something fruity at Delaney's Delectables along with the tiramisu. Summer elves loved fruit.

He shook his head as if amused with himself and started rolling again. "I'll bring wine. Red okay?"

"Red's great." I was huffing a little, to my embarrassment. Hey, the rug was a beast. Heavy *and* large. And Juniper had hustled me out of the house so fast this morning that I'd had time for only one Dr Pepper. I would have grabbed a doughnut, too, but I was out of them.

The thought of sugar made my stomach rumble. I was starving, actually.

Cooper lifted the roll over his shoulder like it was nothing. Clearly, he'd had breakfast. My end flopped to the ground behind him like a giant sausage. Not that food was the only thing on my mind. He glanced back at me. "You'd better get that unless you want me to drag it all the way to my truck."

"Right. On it." I hoisted the trailing part onto my shoulder and followed him to his vehicle. Since I was connected to him by the rug, I was sort of on autopilot. Mostly because I was staring at his very tight backside. It was impossible not to, what with it being right in front of me and all.

But that little trip was enough to show me that no matter what I was telling myself, I was not beyond the reach of Cooper Sullivan's charms.

I definitely still liked him. Way more than I wanted to admit.

Cooper offered to help me set up the rug, so I let him. I might have mentioned that thing was heavy. And getting it into place required furniture to be moved. But wow, did it make a difference in the way my apartment looked. Really gave it a homier vibe. I hadn't realized just how bland it had been until now.

Once the rug was taken care of, I thanked him profusely, then shooed him off as quickly and politely as I could. Getting the new stuff situated would have been easier with his help, but being around him was clogging my head with thoughts I wasn't ready to deal with.

Such as how much I liked him. *And* how much I liked Greyson.

A girl could like two guys, right? I certainly thought it ought to be allowed. Especially after all my years of liking no one in the North Pole.

Cooper didn't seem to be upset at me for showing him the door. He knew I had work to do and we were seeing each other for dinner. Hopefully, between now and then, I could get my head on straight. One thing that might help was dealing with the rest of the stuff I'd brought home. At the very least, it was a distraction.

I put the pillows on the couch as artfully as I could, positioned the decorative box on the coffee table (promising myself I'd test my lock-picking skills after everything else was tackled, including the paperwork awaiting me in the office downstairs) and went to work hanging the robe hook. That wasn't too hard. Juniper had lent me her toolbox a couple days ago and it had an assortment of screws and nails in a little plastic container. I found two screws the right size, got it level and secured it in place.

Spider's incredible velvet Elvis was next. That took almost no effort. One nail, a few taps of the hammer and his meal area was totally swagged out. Okay, maybe not totally. I still needed to buy him a snazzy placemat to go under his dishes to complete the ensemble. "Spider, come see how pretty your dining room looks."

He was sitting on the new rug, swatting at one of his many catnip-scented toys that I'd tossed there.

"Spider. Seriously. Come over here."

He ignored me, took the toy in his mouth and trotted off toward the bedroom. He liked to hide his toys under the bed. I'd found twelve of them under there last month while looking for a shoe.

I gave up on him temporarily. It was time to hang the big picture over the sofa. That took more work than I anticipated. And I have to confess, this hammer-and-nails business is not my forte. The first time I attempted to put the painting up, my measurements were a little off and the bottom of the frame touched the top of the couch.

I measured again, tapped the nails in, hung the painting and hoped for the best. The best being the picture hiding the extra holes in the wall.

Fingers crossed, I jumped off the couch and stepped back. Yep. The mistake was hidden. I nodded at my handiwork. The place was really coming together. And now that I had the rug and the tropical landscape, I had a color scheme. Green and blue with tan.

The magical snow globe I used to communicate with my dad looked completely out of place on the table next to the sofa, but that couldn't be helped. It stayed. Magic was about the only way I could reach him since electronics were unreliable in the North Pole.

But the hula salt and pepper shakers definitely worked. And I could order some more things, like a comfy throw for the back of the couch and maybe a runner for the kitchen table and even a valance for the big window that led to the fire escape.

Look at me getting all domestic. And it wasn't even nine A.M. yet. That had to be some kind of personal record.

As impressed with myself as I was, I had yet to eat or shower, and at some point, I needed to get down to my office and take over the magic running the Snow Saturday. *My office.* If I can be honest, that still sounded odd to my ears. Odd in a good way. I grinned. I liked the ring of it, and after all the work that had gone into cleaning it up and organizing it so that it made sense to me, I was proud of the space.

Toly, the previous manager (and one of my uncle Kris's former tinkers), had used the office as a workshop space for his toy designs (in addition to usual office activities), and as a result it had overflowed with papers and drawings and half-completed models.

But I'd put in the sweat equity and earned the right to call it mine. I'd cleaned it out, painted it and transformed it into something efficient and welcoming. A place I didn't mind spending time. Which was why I was ready to go down there and get some work done.

I gave Spider his second breakfast, grabbed a Dr Pepper and jumped in the shower. Yes, I drink pop in the shower. I'm a multitasker. I still hadn't eaten, so I didn't stand under the water as long as I would have liked. I dried my hair and dressed in what I liked to call business casual, which meant a sundress and sandals. I was getting the hang of summer in Georgia—no small feat for a winter elf.

I was just finishing my makeup when I heard a loud crash. It was followed by a loud meow and then the thundering of little cat feet through my living room. I rolled my eyes. It was still too early for this amount of crazy. "I wish I had a never-ending supply of Dr Pepper. That would make this nuttiness easier to take."

But I didn't and I was going to have to deal with whatever mess Spider had made in my current only partially caffeinated state.

"Spider, what have you done now?" I called out. Shaking my head, I walked into the living room to survey the damage. The decorative box I'd just bought was on the floor. The top lay a few feet away, the hinges…unhinged. "So much for picking the lock."

Spider sat on the windowsill, licking his foot and pretending he knew nothing.

I narrowed my eyes at him. "You silly creature. What gets into you, huh? Was it the catnip? Do you need a twelve-step program? I wish you could talk. Then at least you could explain yourself."

He stopped mid-lick like he'd blown a fuse, eyes wide and staring at nothing, then after a second he went right back to cleaning.

Who could understand cats? I sighed as I turned and squatted to examine the box. Empty, just as I'd suspected. Although there was an odd green iridescence to the inside of it. Almost like the powder off a butterfly's wings. I studied the hinges. I supposed they could be repaired. Spider was still a stinker. I shook my head. "Thanks for getting the top off, you rascal."

"You're welcome," a male voice said.

I froze. I was alone in the apartment. Or at least I thought I was. I spun around, staying in a crouched position. Still alone, as far as I could tell. I got up, put the box and lid on the kitchen table and ran to the window, throwing it open to check the fire escape.

No one there, although I thought I heard the faintest tinny laugh fading away.

"Okay, that was *weird*."

Spider rubbed against my arm. "What's weird?"

I whipped around to look at him. It was possible that rising early had caused me to split with reality. Or maybe it was my lack of sugar. Had he just said that? Couldn't be. He was a cat. I laughed it off. Or tried to. "You can't talk, right?"

He lifted his little head and looked right at me. "Nope."

"Good, because—yikes!" I jumped back. "Son of a nutcracker, why are you talking? Have you always been able to talk? Am I losing my mind? I need sugar, don't I?"

He canted his head at me, like he didn't understand.

I took a breath and repeated the question I was most interested in having answered. "Have you always been able to talk?"

"No."

"Then why now?"

"That's what Mama wished for." He started licking the other foot.

"Mama? Who's Mama? Wait, am I Mama?"

He paused and looked at me. "Mama."

"Are you saying you granted my wish? Are you a genie?"

That got his attention. "No genie, cat." He lay down. "Spider tired."

Just like that, he was out.

"Hang on, buster. No going to sleep in the middle of this. Did you grant the wish?"

One eye came open. "That salmon cat food is yucky."

"Focus. Who granted the wish?"

He closed his eye, did a big sigh and went back to sleep.

I took that to mean he didn't know. I stood there for a long time, staring at him, trying to make sense of what had just happened.

I couldn't. The best I could do was...my cat could talk because someone had granted my wish that he could.

Who that someone was, I had no clue. Well, it wasn't a genie. According to my *talking* cat. I needed food. And sugar. Fast.

I grabbed my purse and headed for the elevator. I went straight downstairs to the warehouse, past my office and into the store, where big fat flakes of magical snow were drifting to the floor and disappearing without leaving a single drop of water.

Juniper was working with Kip, one of the two new employees. He was working the floor, so that gave me a chance to talk to her since she was behind the register.

She smiled at me. "Get everything situated? And, more importantly, do any kissing?"

I shook my head and was about to speak when she said, "You don't look so hot." She leaned toward me. "And why do you only have mascara on one eye?"

The mascara thing was perplexing, but not as much as what had just happened. I sidled up next to her behind the counter and hissed, "Spider can talk."

She squinted at me. "What did you say?"

"My *cat* can *talk*."

She pressed a hand to my head. "You feel okay? Are you putting too much effort into the snow, because I can handle this if you need to—"

"I'm serious. And I haven't even begun to help

with the snow. Listen, I don't know what happened, but he can talk. He said it's because my wish was granted."

Juniper turned and smiled as a woman came into the store.

She stopped at the counter. "Do you have that new game, Bobbles?"

Juniper pointed toward the game section. "Yes, ma'am. You'll find that in with puzzles and games, to the right of the dolls."

"Thank you."

The woman left, and Juniper's smile disappeared as she whipped around to face me. "You need to start from the beginning."

I told her the whole thing, about the crash and the box and what I'd said and what Spider had said. "I'm freaking out."

"I would be too." She tapped her fingers on the counter. "Do you think there was a genie in that box?"

I made a face. "Are you making fun of me?"

"No! There could have been."

"Seriously?"

"You just told me your cat can talk because your wish was granted. Are you not seeing the connection?"

I sighed. "I just didn't think genies were real."

She snorted softly. "You remember where you live now, right? This is Nocturne Falls. Also, can I just remind you that your uncle is Santa Claus? You of all people should know anything is possible."

She had a point. I took a breath and put both hands on the counter. "So…a genie. That would explain what happened. But shouldn't I have seen the genie? Shouldn't there have been a puff of smoke or something?"

She shrugged. "I don't know how this stuff works. It's not always how it is in the movies. But if it is, you might have two wishes left."

"I need to be careful what I say in my apartment, then." I rubbed my forehead. I wouldn't want some offhand comment to become my next reality. Unless it was wishing for a lifetime supply of chocolate doughnuts. Can you imagine if they all showed up at once? What a way to die. I refocused on the matter at hand. "Why would anyone sell a box with a genie in it?"

"Maybe they didn't know? It could have been locked the whole time. That woman Bryn said the owners collected things from their travels. And if they were supernaturals, which is a fairly high probability in this town, there's no telling what kind of places and shops they might have been to."

"Very true. I think I need to find out who the owners were."

Juniper nodded, smiling at another entering

customer. "That would be a good starting place. And you know who could help you with that?"

"Greyson?"

She rolled her eyes. "Cooper. He's a fireman. Firemen know who lives where. Or they can at least find out."

"Yeah, I suppose. He'll be over for dinner tonight, as you know. I can wait until then. I mean, this whole thing could be temporary." I didn't want Cooper to think I was making excuses to talk to him. Maybe I'd text Greyson instead. Just as soon as I left the shop.

"Maybe, but it might be fun if it wasn't. You'd never get lonely. So long as Spider isn't super chatty." Juniper gave me a little shrug. "This is Nocturne Falls, Jayne. You have to expect the unexpected."

"I suppose you're right. And it's not like Spider got turned into a giant version of his namesake or anything. Talking's not so bad."

"Exactly." She crossed her arms. "You going to be okay?"

"Yeah, I'll figure it out. I'll be in my office most of the day. Right after I get some breakfast at Mummy's. I feel the need for something supremely over the top."

She smiled sweetly. "Maybe go put some mascara on that other eye first."

"Good call." I smiled back. "Thanks for talking

me down. I'll let you know when I get back from breakfast. You want anything?"

"No, I ate before I came in. Thanks, though." She turned to help a customer who'd come up to the counter. I made my exit, heading back to the apartment.

Spider was still asleep, and I felt a little strange being happy about that. I loved my cat. But the talking was weird. Well, maybe it wasn't the talking that bothered me so much as not knowing why he could suddenly communicate. I'd feel better once I knew for sure what had happened.

Which was where Greyson came in. I pulled out my phone.

Breakfast at Mummy's in ten minutes. You in?

I went to add mascara to my naked lashes. He texted back as I was slipping the tube back into my makeup bag.

Morning, love. I'm in. See you there.

I grinned. The only thing better than devouring a plate of Mummy's chocolate-chip banana pancakes was devouring them with Greyson.

Greyson didn't technically meet me at Mummy's since I arrived ahead of him. No big deal. I got a table and ordered a Dr Pepper while I waited.

He was only a few minutes behind me, and in a way, I was glad I'd gotten there first. Gave me a great seat from which to watch and enjoy his entrance. He sauntered through the restaurant in his typical getup, which was sort of a darkly romantic, slightly Gothic look with a little Victorian flair thrown in—black leather pants with a lace-up fly, a billowy white shirt, and tall black boots, along with his usual pile of silver necklaces, rings and bracelets.

Mixed in with those necklaces was a black leather cord holding a little pouch. I was pretty sure his ability to walk in daylight came from whatever magical ingredients that pouch contained.

It wasn't hard to see why he'd been hired to play one of the characters who roamed Nocturne Falls' streets, taking pictures with tourists and generally adding to the Halloween-every-day vibe that earned the town its dollars. Not only did he look the part of the Vampire On Duty, he exuded an air of dangerous sex appeal that was exactly what you'd expect from one of the undead.

He was the quintessential vampire. And more Aidan Turner than Johnny Depp these days, but I was a hundred percent all right with that.

He leaned in and kissed my cheek before taking the seat across from me. "You look lovely."

Sure, now that I had mascara'd both eyes. I smiled. "And you look roguishly handsome as always."

"You flatter me." But he smiled back, clearly pleased.

He had to know he looked good, because if I wasn't oblivious to the admiring stares he drew from the other restaurant patrons, then he wasn't either.

The server showed up almost instantly. Greyson always got good service. She handed him a menu. "Morning, doll. What can I get for you?"

"Coffee." He kept his gaze on me a second longer before looking at her. "Thank you."

"Coming right up. I'll be right back to take your orders." She twittered away.

He slid his hand across the table and laid it over

mine. "How are you, my love? I was starting to think I'd lost your favor."

"No. Definitely not that. I've just been swamped with work." As I mentioned, I hadn't seen a lot of Cooper lately, but I hadn't seen much of Greyson either.

He nodded. "How's the transition going?"

"Good so far."

"The new employees working out, then?"

"Very well. Kip's a fast learner, and Holly is a little quiet, but a good worker. They're both fitting in well. The third and final employee should be arriving next week."

"I'm glad to hear it. Then maybe you'll be free for dinner more often."

"Maybe." I smiled as the server returned to take our order.

She beamed at Greyson. Naturally. "What can I get you, hon?"

"Steak, rare, three eggs, over easy, home fries and biscuits." He handed her the menu.

"You got it, sugar." After a long second, the waitress turned to me. "And for you?"

"Full stack of the banana chocolate-chip pancakes with whipped cream and a side of bacon. Oh, and I need a cinnamon bun to go. Extra frosting." I turned over my menu to her as well.

"Coming up." She left us, menus tucked under her arm.

Greyson popped a brow. "You're going to need a shot of insulin after a breakfast like that."

I grinned. "I can handle my sugar. The cinnamon bun isn't for me, though. It's for Juniper. Who can also handle her sugar." Juniper might have said she didn't want anything, but I knew her well enough to know she wouldn't turn down a cinnamon bun from Mummy's. "I owe her after she took me to this great estate sale this morning."

"Oh? Did some shopping, did you?"

I sipped my Dr Pepper. "I did. Got some great stuff for my place. That's part of why I asked you to breakfast."

"Did you buy me a present now?"

I narrowed my eyes at him, my mouth pursed in mock judgment. "Are you saying my company isn't already a gift?"

He laughed. "It's all I could ever want and more."

"Good answer. I was actually hoping you might know who lived at the house that was holding the sale. It's that Victorian with the turret on Phantom Lane. The one with the big wraparound front porch."

He smirked. "That describes almost all the houses on Phantom Lane. That whole neighborhood is old Victorians. But I know the one you mean, since the only one for sale recently was the Greshams' place. What do you need to know about them?"

I kept my voice low. "Were they supernaturals?"

He hesitated. "After a fashion."

"What's that mean?"

"She did some card reading on the side, but it wasn't anything serious. More of a party trick, really. But he was a psychometrist."

I scrunched up my face in confusion. "Translation?"

Greyson put his hands out in front of him like he was holding something. "Roger Gresham claimed he could read objects. Tell you a thing's history just by touching it. True or not, it's what drove the success of their shop."

"Their shop?" As suspected, my favorite vampire was a wealth of information.

"They had a curiosity shop here in town. Then, about a year ago, he apparently fell in love with another woman, filed for divorce, and left town with his new flame for life in Sedona, Arizona. Francine was heartbroken and closed the business down. But the house only went up for sale a few months ago."

Greyson leaned in. "I think too, that without Roger to read objects, the shop lost some of its appeal. Or maybe Francine just didn't have it in her to be surrounded by all those things that reminded her of the man who'd broken her heart. Either way, she's become a bit of a recluse lately. On a rare occasion, you might see her at the Shop-n-Save, but that's it. Otherwise, she rarely leaves that house. But I guess she must be moving now that the house has sold."

I nodded. "Everything inside looked pretty much packed up. Where was their store?"

"Their old shop was where Delaney's Delectables is now. It housed an insurance agency briefly, but they moved to a larger space and then it sat empty until Delaney took it over."

"Huh." I sat back. "I love that place, so I can't say I wish the Greshams still had their shop, but it's so sad that her husband did that to her." I knew what it was like to feel betrayed by a man. Even if that betrayal had really been a big mix-up. Still, I crossed my arms and narrowed my gaze. "*Men*."

His brows lifted. "Am I being included in that scurrilous company?"

I smiled. "No. But I'm keeping my eye on you."

He grinned. "A lad can dream."

"How do you know all this?"

He flashed a smile. "Birdie Caruthers, the sheriff's aunt. She's also the receptionist at the sheriff's department and I help out with events once in a while. Crowd control, that sort of thing. Birdie likes me. And she likes to talk."

What woman didn't like him? Besides Juniper. "And you obviously like to listen."

His smile stayed put. "Information is a powerful thing."

"True enough."

The server returned with our monstrous plates of food, and we spent the next few minutes attacking it. Well, I attacked. Greyson ate with gusto, but only one of us ended up with syrup in their hair. And it wasn't him. In my defense, the butter was really far away.

As I dipped my napkin into my water glass to work on my sticky tresses, Greyson rested his knife on the edge of his plate. "You didn't say why you want to know about the Greshams. Is there more to your line of questioning?"

"Yes!" How had I forgotten? Chocolate-chip banana pancakes were very distracting, that's how. "Do you think Francine might have been selling stuff from the shop at the estate sale? Like, supernatural stuff? Because one of things I picked up seems like it might have done...*something* to Spider."

"Many of their things were of a supernatural bent, so it's possible. And yes, I'm sure a lot of the items up for sale today were left over from the shop. What exactly did you buy, and what did it do to your cat?"

I lowered my voice and leaned in. "I bought this fancy decorative box, which Spider proceeded to knock off the coffee table in one of his catnip-induced rampages through the apartment. Anyway, I thought the top was stuck on, but the fall cracked it open, and now he can talk."

"Spider?"

"Yep." I stabbed a hunk of pancake.

"You mean he meows a lot?"

"No, I mean he spoke to me."

Greyson blinked a few times. "Your cat can talk. In actual words. English words."

I nodded. "Yep. I swear on my uncle's beard."

"And you think the box and this new…ability are related."

I shrugged one shoulder. "I can't think of what else might have caused it. There's some green iridescent powder inside the box. Like a magical dust maybe? Or the residue of a spell. Or some other kind of magical thing. That's really all I have to go on. I figured if I could talk to whoever owned the box and find out what was in there, I'd at least know what I'm dealing with."

Greyson nodded. "Francine might see you. She's not exactly the type that takes visitors, but this is a special case."

"I'd say. Having a talking cat is a little unnerving."

He picked up his fork again, this time going after his home fries. "I know someone who might be able to get you in to see her."

"Who's that?"

He downed a mouthful of potatoes before answering. "The most connected werewolf I know. My good friend, Birdie Caruthers."

Half an hour later, despite the paperwork waiting for me back at the office, I walked into the sheriff's department with Greyson so he could introduce me to Birdie. No time like the present and all that. The takeout bag containing Juniper's cinnamon roll hung from my hand. Greyson had gotten another one as a gift for the woman we'd come to see.

The older woman behind the reception desk, who I assumed was Birdie, was on the phone. "You don't say?" She gasped. "Are you certain? Well, bless her heart, that is highly unusual. I don't see how a deputy can help, but I'll send someone over. Yes, right away. All right. Y'all take care now. Bye-bye."

She hung up and turned to us, her face lighting up with a big smile when she saw Greyson. "Well, now, Greyson Garrett. This is an unexpected pleasure. What brings you in here? Did you get called in for something? Because if you did, no one said a word to me about it."

"No, I didn't get called in. But I did bring you a cinnamon roll from Mummy's." He put the container on the counter in front of her.

"That was so thoughtful! You know how I love those things." She popped open the container and inhaled. "Oh, that's going to ruin my lunch and I don't even care." She closed it and set it aside. "Now I was born at night, but it wasn't last night, so out with it. What exactly are you after?"

He touched his hand to his chest. "I'd say I'm insulted that you think so little of me, but I appreciate a woman who gets to the heart of it." He shifted his hand to my shoulder. "I wanted you to meet a friend of mine. She's new in town. And since I know how much you like Christmas, I thought you ought to meet her. This is Jayne Frost, new manager of Santa's Workshop Toy Store."

Birdie's eyes lit up, and she stood to shake my hand. "It is so nice to meet you. I've heard about you. You're a real live princess, aren't you?"

"I am."

"Ooo," Birdie exclaimed. "I've never met royalty before. Unless you count Myrtis Lobb the Peach Cobbler Queen, which I do not. What's it like being a princess?"

"It's...very nice. There are a lot fewer jewels than you'd imagine."

"I've also heard Santa Claus is your uncle." Birdie shook her head. "I can't even. The North Pole sounds so magical."

"He is, and it is. But then, so is Nocturne Falls." And it was getting more magical by the moment.

Greyson cleared his throat. "Birdie, Jayne

bought something at Francine Gresham's estate sale this morning and would like a chance to talk to Francine about it. We thought you might be able to make that happen."

Birdie sat back down. "I do know Francine, but she's not much on visitors these days."

"It's sort of a royal emergency," I lied.

Birdie's brows shot up. "Oh?"

I thought fast as I leaned in closer. "I think something I picked up at her sale, a fancy box she used to own, has somehow put a spell on my cat allowing him to talk. Of course, my sweet little Spider would never share official North Pole information, but he's overheard conversations between my father, Jack Frost, and me. I'd hate to think what might happen if word got out about Spider. Someone might kidnap him and force him to reveal all." I shook my head. "Can you imagine if one of my uncle Kris's proprietary secrets got out? It could ruin Christmas!"

Birdie had been nodding along as I'd unraveled that tangled thread. She clucked her tongue. "That would be awful. Just awful. I'll see what I can do about taking you to visit Francine."

"Thank you." Who said I couldn't act?

"Very kind of you, Birdie," Greyson added.

She gave us a curious look. "You said you bought the box this morning?"

"Yes."

41

"And that's when your cat suddenly developed the ability to talk?"

"Right after I got it home and he knocked the top off."

"You're sure it's related to the box?"

"I guess. I mean, he started talking immediately after the box fell off the table. Why?"

She glanced at the phone. "Piper Hodges, her family owns the local newspaper, the Tombstone, got out of the shower at the gym to find that she'd turned blue."

"Blue?" Greyson repeated.

Birdie nodded. "As Princess Jayne's hair. Oh! I was supposed to send a deputy over there. Hang on." She snatched up the radio next to her phone. "Deputy Blythe, this is Birdie, come in."

The radio crackled, and a female voice answered. "Go ahead, Birdie."

"Can you swing by the Tombstone? Piper Hodges turned blue this morning, and her mother wants a deputy to take a report."

A few seconds passed before Deputy Blythe responded. "Did you say she turned blue?"

"I did."

"How about that," Deputy Blythe said. "On my way. Over and out."

Birdie put the radio down. "Like I was saying, your cat being able to talk isn't the only strange thing that's happened this morning, but then, this is Nocturne Falls. You just never know in a town like this." She sighed. "I'll reach out to Francine and see what I can set up. Leave me your number, and I'll call you when I know something."

I pulled out one of my brand new business cards and handed it over. Right there under *Jayne Frost, Manager* was my cell number. "Thank you so much. I really appreciate it."

"I'm happy to help. My nephew, Charlie, loves to visit your shop and seeing you is a good reminder that I haven't taken him in a while. I'll see you soon, I'm sure."

"Soon, then."

Greyson and I said good-bye and were back on the sidewalk a few moments later. I turned to him as we headed for the store and my apartment. "What if this doesn't have anything to do with the box? What if whatever caused that woman to turn blue is behind Spider's new language skills?"

He seemed to think that over for a second. "Could be. But the reverse could also be true. What if the reason Spider can talk is also the reason Piper turned blue?"

"I don't know. Spider said it was because I'd wished for it. I definitely didn't wish for a woman I've never met to change colors."

He snorted softly. "I certainly hope not."

Greyson walked me to the warehouse door and said good-bye to me there with a too-brief kiss. While I replayed that, I went through the vestibule that held the Nocturne Falls employees' only elevator (off limits to everyone else since it led down to a secret area of the town) and into the warehouse that held all the stock for the toy store, the employee break room, my office and the elevator that led to the apartments above.

I thought about going up to mine for a moment, maybe see if Spider was still talking, but I was already overdue to start my paperwork. There was only one more thing to take care of before I got those inventory sheets under control.

I veered right and straight into the shop. I could sense the magic in play that was causing the snow to fall in the store. I wove my own through it, taking on the heavy lifting of the shimmer, which was what we called that kind of magic.

Juniper was at the counter bagging a family's items. I waited until she was done and the family was on their way out to put the bag from Mummy's into her hands. "Here you go."

She closed her eyes and inhaled. "Cinnamon roll. And I didn't even ask."

"Yep."

She grinned and tucked the bag under the counter. "You're the best. And I'm not just saying that because you're my boss now."

I laughed. "Sure. How's it going? You need me for anything?"

"Nope, we're good. I felt you take on some of the shimmer. Thanks for that."

I looked toward the back of the store. "And Kip? How's he doing?"

"Kip is great. I think he's ready to be on the register."

"Go ahead and let him, then. You're here, so if he runs into any issues, you can help him."

"You got it. You headed into your office?"

I nodded. "I'm hoping to do four hours' worth of paperwork in two. Think I can?"

"I don't know." She cocked her head, a coy look on her face. "Does that include schedules for next week?"

I groaned. "Make that five hours of paperwork. I

forgot about that. Which reminds me, I need to see what's going on with our new hire."

"Guy or girl?"

"I don't know. My dad was supposed to tell me today." And just like that, I did have to run back up to the apartment. "Okay, if you need me, you know where to find me."

Juniper gave me a thumbs-up as Kip came up to the counter.

I gave them both a wave. "Later."

I left them to their work and about two minutes later was walking into my place. Spider wasn't immediately visible, which meant he was probably sleeping in one of his current favorite spots, the walk-in closet or the bathroom sink.

I opened the fridge to get a Dr Pepper and stopped mid-reach. The six-pack was full. I could have sworn I'd only left five bottles in there this morning. I'd taken the sixth one into the shower. Had I imagined that?

I closed the fridge and checked my recycling bin. The empty bottle sat right on top. Huh. That was weird. But right on track for how today was going.

I got my drink and headed for the couch and my snow globe. I twisted off the top of the DP and took a long sip as I shook the globe.

The snow flew, and some seconds later, my dad's face appeared. "Hi, honey. How's it going?"

"Good. How are you and Mom?"

"We're great. And it's good to hear from you, but I don't have too much time to talk, unfortunately. I have to meet your uncle at the stables to look at how training the new reindeer is going."

"No problem. Tell Uncle Kris I said hi."

He smiled. "You must have called about something. What is it, honey? I can spare a few minutes."

"I'll be quick. Does ER have the name of the new employee yet?" I'd sent three acceptable possibilities last week to Elf Resources. It was their job to figure out who was the most available and where they were on the wait list, then contact whoever was in the top spot, give them the good news and make all the necessary arrangements. Being a Santa's Workshop employee was a pretty sought-after job.

"Not yet. I'll get that for you by next week, I promise. Even if I have to go down there myself."

I grinned. "That'll shake them up." Not that my dad wasn't a hands-on kind of guy. He was, but anytime the Winter King paid a personal visit to a department, it was a notable event.

"Anything else?"

"Any chance I can get another snow globe? Now that the office is mine, it would be nice to have one down there too. It would make it easier for me to contact you instead of having to run up to my apartment all the time."

He nodded. "Good idea. I'll send one through the Santa's Bag today. I'll make sure the box has your name on it so it's not mixed up with any inventory."

"Cool. Thanks."

"You're welcome." He hesitated. "I do need to get going, but since I have you, there's something I wanted to talk to you about."

"Sure."

He smiled. "Your mom and I know you can't come home. You're too busy. But we'd like to come for a visit." He held his hands up. "Not immediately. You're still settling in, and we don't want to complicate that process for you. But maybe in a month. You don't have to answer now, just give it some thought and let me know."

"I don't need to think about it. There's plenty of room for you in the guest apartment. And Mom would love some of the stores here." It would be great to see them. I had a good relationship with my parents, and it would be a lie to say I didn't miss them. "A month from now sounds good. Things will be much smoother in a few more weeks."

And maybe Spider wouldn't be talking by then. Because I could only imagine what kinds of things he might say to my parents. *Jayne eats doughnuts for dinner.* Or, *That vampire your daughter likes to kiss brought me a nice catnip mouse.*

Yeah. *No.*

"Great," my dad said. "Your mom will be happy to hear that. Do you need anything else?"

"No, I'm good." They'd already sent the rest of my summer clothes, which wasn't much, through the Santa's Bag. "I bought some stuff for the apartment with the money you sent me. Much appreciated."

"Happy to do it. If you need extra—"

"Nope. My salary is more than enough."

He laughed softly. "Jay, you're the Winter Princess. It's okay to ask. Or want. You don't even have a car."

"No, but I have the company bikes in the warehouse, and if I need to go farther, I just call iRyde." Not that I had any plans to be spending money on that service for a while. "Besides, we both know my driver's license is a poor indicator of my ability to drive." It was really just for identification purposes, having been obtained in a somewhat magical manner. Technically, I wasn't even a resident of Alaska.

Now, a sleigh pulled by reindeer? I could hold my own against just about any other winter elf who wanted to challenge me to that race.

"All right, honey. But promise me that if you need something, you'll ask."

"I will. Love you. Go meet Uncle Kris before he tracks you down."

"On my way. Love you too."

The snow settled, and he was gone.

I sighed happily and picked up my Dr Pepper. It would be fun to show my parents my new hometown.

I was about to head out when I got the urge to check on Spider. Maybe the talking thing had been a temporary fluke. Like a weird drift of random magic had caught him. As I'd heard several times this morning, anything was possible in this town.

I walked toward the bedroom to look in the closet. "Spider?"

A sleepy meow answered me.

I found him on the shoe shelf second up from the floor. The shelf was empty, because even with the new pairs of flip-flops I'd recently purchased, I didn't have enough shoes to fill it. He rolled over to look at me upside down. Maybe he was back to being a regular cat. "Hey, baby." I rubbed his now-exposed tummy. "Just checking on you."

He closed his eyes and purred. "Spider likes scratches."

So much for that. "You talking is weird. I just have to say that."

He stopped purring and looked at me. "No more talking?"

"No, that doesn't seem fair to you. I guess you

don't have any more thoughts on how this happened, huh?"

The purring started up again as I scratched under his chin, causing his answer to vibrate out of him. "No-o-o-o."

"Okay, worth a shot." I stood up. "I have to go to the office. Cooper will be coming over for dinner, just so you know."

Spider didn't say anything. He was either asleep or didn't care. Either way, I was starting to feel very much like I had a roommate.

Once I got to my office, settled behind my desk and dug into the workload that needed doing, Spider's newfound ability was temporarily forgotten. Work was good for clearing the mind of all other thoughts. Or at least, pushing them off to a dark corner.

I decided to do the schedule tomorrow. I didn't have the name of the new employee or when they were arriving, anyway. The inventories weren't anything major, just lots of checking and double-checking to make sure my order sheets were right.

Once those were done, I put them in an official correspondence envelope (red eight-and-a-half-by-eleven) and walked it to the Santa's Bag.

Every Santa's Workshop had one. Naturally, the original was carried by my uncle Kris on Christmas Eve, but these were modeled after that one and used the same magic. They were the same shape and size, about three feet by four feet—if a red velvet sack could be measured that way. And they were bigger on the inside. Much bigger. Like a TARDIS.

But no, Uncle Kris is not a Time Lord. Just stopping that rumor before it starts.

The bags always kept their upright shape too, although it was easy to see when there was something in them. If they were full, they bulged. Even if it was one tiny block or a solitary sheet of paper. If they were empty, the sides sagged inward.

Ours was empty at the moment. I loosened the golden drawstring around the top, opened the sack and dropped the envelope in.

The sides puffed out with a soft whoosh, then slumped in again as someone on the North Pole side took out my envelope. In a day or two, our bag would be full with the orders I'd just sent through.

I tied the bag up and was a few steps away when I heard the whoosh again. I looked back to see the sides bulging.

When I dug into the sack, I found a large box with my name on it. I smiled at my mom's swirly handwriting.

I grabbed the box, which was surprisingly heavy, and took it back to my office. It wasn't even halfway open when I smelled the sugar. My mother had sent goodies. My mouth started to water as I took out the first of three containers.

Number one held my mom's famous snickerdoodle toffee cookies. You haven't had cookies until you've had cookies baked by Santa Claus's sister. Not saying my aunt Martha can't bake—she totally can. But my mom's cookies are kind of world class. How do you think my uncle Kris developed such a hankering for them?

Container number two was heavy with eggnog fudge. That was Aunt Martha's specialty, and it was like Christmas in your mouth. I felt all warm inside knowing my family had thought of me. Obviously, they'd been planning to send me a care package. Me asking for another snow globe was just a happy coincidence.

Container three was the second snow globe. I unwound the bubble wrap keeping it safe and found a little handwritten note on my dad's official stationery. *This means we're going to talk more, you know.*

I laughed. "I know."

I set it on the corner of my desk, next to the picture of my parents. It looked nice there, even if an empty snow globe was a little odd.

Work—bills this time—kept me occupied until Juniper stuck her head in. "Hey, you busy? I don't want to interrupt."

"No, I can take a break. What's up?"

"Just wanted to see if you needed anything from the Shop-n-Save for your dinner tonight with Cooper. I'm going to run over there since my shift is over."

I looked at the time. "It's five o'clock? Snowballs, I did not mean to work that long." I jumped up and grabbed my purse. The goodies could stay in my office, especially because I'd eaten the last of my gummy bears while doing my paperwork. "I do need stuff for dinner tonight, but I'll go with you. The rest of this can wait until tomorrow."

"Excellent."

We took two company bikes and rode to the grocery store. Ten minutes later, we were in the aisles and filling a buggy. Not too much, of course, but the company bikes had baskets, so between us we'd have no problem getting everything home.

And I'd made my life easier by buying most of Spider's necessities at the pet store down the street from the warehouse. It was a little more expensive, but the convenience factor outweighed the cost bump. You try biking while balancing a twenty-pound jug of litter. Nothing about living in the North Pole prepared me for that.

I tossed a box of spaghetti into the cart, then picked out a jar of sauce. "Have you talked to Pete lately?"

Juniper nodded. "We're going to Café Claude this weekend."

"Oh, excellent. It's a great place."

Juniper pushed the buggy as we walked to the meat counter. "It's kind of spendy, though, isn't it?"

"It's not that bad. And Pete's a pharmacist. I think they make decent money." I nudged her. "Speaking of, I'm promoting you to first-shift manager. And Buttercup to second-shift manager. You'll both be getting a raise."

Juni let out a little squeal. "That's awesome, thank you!"

I grinned. It was nice to be able to do that. Definitely one of the perks of the job. "It'll be effective this pay period."

"I'm so happy. Thanks!"

"You both earned it. And frankly, you were overdue." I picked up a pack of ground beef to add to the sauce. Cooper was a big guy with an appetite to match. I couldn't invite him over for dinner and not feed him something substantial. "I need garlic bread and one of those summer fruit tarts from the bakery."

She turned the cart in that direction. "Don't you think the ones from Delaney's are better?"

"Definitely, but I worked too long and don't have time to run down there now." The tiramisu would have to wait. "And I'm not trying to impress

Cooper too much. This is just a thanks for his help this morning, not a let's-get-back-together dinner."

"Oh, right. I forgot that you're pretending you don't like him as much as you do."

I shot her a look as we walked into the baked-goods section. "I can see that promotion has gone right to your head."

She stuck her tongue out at me and went to get some breakfast pastries while I picked out a berry tart and a loaf of ready-made parmesan garlic bread.

We grabbed a few more things, hit the checkout and were cycling home a few minutes later. We parted in the hall, each of us loaded down with bags that made unlocking our doors harder than normal.

I got my stuff inside and set my bags on the kitchen counter. "Spider, I'm home." It seemed like the thing to do. I heard a meow in return.

I unpacked my groceries. Besides the fixings for the evening's dinner, I'd gotten a dozen chocolate doughnuts (naturally), three trays of frozen mac-n-cheese, which was my current food rut, some nice cheese and a box of wheat crackers. I figured I could put the cheese and crackers out for an appetizer.

Biking had made me sweaty (the fact that it was August in Georgia was also a contributing factor), so I went to shower and freshen up.

As I was about to strip down and jump into the hot water, Spider strolled in. "Spider hungry."

"I'm about to get naked here."

"What's naked?"

"You know…nothing but skin covering you. Er, fur."

"Is Spider naked?"

"Uh…sort of." I wasn't mentally prepared to have this conversation with my cat. "What did you want again?"

He let out a loud yowl. "Hungry."

"All right, let's go fix that." I walked to the little spot at the end of the kitchen counter where his feeding station was set up to see what he needed. The velvet Elvis really did snazz it up. Spider's dry food bowl was pretty full, but he'd eaten through the bits in the middle so that the bottom of the bowl was visible. I gave it a little shake to redistribute the kibble.

He trotted over and looked inside. "Thanks." Then he started eating.

I rolled my eyes and went to take my shower, fairly certain that Spider's ability to talk hadn't made him any smarter. His little cat brain seemed to process things the same way as before. And he clearly didn't care what I was wearing, or not wearing.

I shut the bathroom door anyway. No reason to scar him for life.

The shower was five minutes, tops. When I was done, I chose my outfit to be casual and comfy, but not anything that seemed date-like or flirty. So khaki shorts (another new purchase) and a light blue flowered tank top that matched the highlights in my hair.

Cooper would be here in forty-five minutes. *If* he arrived on time, which he rarely did. Cooper was almost always early.

I put it into overdrive. I got the ground beef cooked and added it to a pot with the sauce to warm. Then I wrapped the bread in foil and put it in the oven on low to do the same thing. That done, I set the table. Nothing fancy. Just dishes, silverware, napkins and sprinkle cheese. Along with my new salt and pepper shakers, of course.

Lastly, I started a big pot of salted water on medium so that as soon as he showed up, I could crank the heat to high, get it boiling and dump the pasta in.

With all that done, I took a quick second to check that my makeup hadn't melted off. The house smelled like an Italian dream, I looked good (casual and cute but not like I was trying too hard), my apartment looked good, and I felt relatively confident that tonight wasn't going to lead to kissing.

Cooper knocked as I left the bathroom. I opened the door. "Hey, you're early. So, right on time."

He smiled and handed me a bottle of red wine and a large bouquet of mixed flowers. "I hope I'm not too early. I stood on the sidewalk for five minutes."

"Thanks for the wine and flowers." I moved out of the way so he could come in. "But you shouldn't have stood out there. You should have come up. We're friends, Coop. No need to be so formal." Maybe I was stressing that point too much, but it couldn't hurt.

"I guess. Smells great in here." He looked around. "And the stuff you bought today really looks good."

"Thanks." I put the wine on the counter and looked for something to put the flowers in. I had a vase leftover from some flowers my parents had sent when I'd gotten bumped on the head trying to rescue one of the store's kidnapped elves.

I pulled that out, filled it with water halfway and stuck the flowers in. They were gorgeous, but I felt a little bad that Cooper had spent money on them and the wine when this dinner was supposed to be about me thanking him.

It was almost like he thought it was a date.

I heard a pop and turned to see Cooper had uncorked the wine.

"Do you have glasses?" he asked. "I think it breathes better if you pour it in advance."

I hadn't planned on drinking tonight. I had

work in the morning, but beyond that, being under the influence of Cooper was hard enough to deal with. I didn't need wine making it worse. "Um, not wine glasses exactly, but there are some in the cabinet there." I pointed. "And really, I can't have more than one glass. Work tomorrow and all that."

He nodded. "Me too."

As he got glasses out, I turned to put the pasta in the water, which was already boiling. "How was your day?"

He laughed. "It was nuts."

"Oh yeah?" I gave the pasta a stir then faced him. The glasses of wine he'd poured were easily equivalent to twice what would have fit into an actual wine glass. I was going to have to pace myself. "What happened?"

He handed me a glass, then leaned on the counter. "What didn't happen? We had a vampire stuck in a coffin, which he claims was a bed when he went to sleep. Then a call for a bird stuck on a roof—"

"How can a bird be stuck on a roof when it can fly?"

"When the bird is actually the mascot for Ricky's Chicken."

"The guy who stands outside the restaurant in the rooster costume waving the sign that says 'Cock-a-doodle-delicious?'"

"That's the guy. Said he had the sudden urge to

climb up on the roof, then couldn't remember why when he got up there. Couldn't get down, either." Cooper sipped his wine. "The whole day was like that. Not a serious call in the bunch."

I gave the pasta another stir. "Did you also respond to Piper Hodges turning blue?"

"No, but we heard about it over dispatch." He shook his head. "Man, today was crazy. And it's not even a full moon."

I took a small sip of my wine. It was good. Fruity and a little sweet. Perfect for summer or winter elves. I debated telling Cooper about Spider, but he was bound to find out before the evening was over. "Yeah, it was pretty weird here too."

As if on cue, Spider walked out, sat in the middle of the living room and yawned.

"Weird how?" Cooper asked.

I gave him the short version of the story, which I was getting pretty good at. "That fancy box I bought? I put it on the coffee table, but Spider knocked it down. Broke the lid off. Right after that, he started to talk."

He turned to look at Spider. "Dude. You can talk?"

Spider walked over to Cooper, rubbed on his leg and then meowed.

Cooper looked at me and raised an eyebrow. "I thought you meant like actual talking. Words."

"He does. He can." I stared at Spider. "Say something."

Spider sauntered away to see if anything new had shown up in his food bowl.

I looked at Cooper. "He really can talk. In English."

The timer dinged, so I pulled the pot off the burner and drained the pasta into the colander waiting in the sink. I gave the strainer a shake, added the pasta to the pot of sauce and stirred it all together.

"Anything I can do to help?" Cooper asked as he walked into the kitchen.

I did a little side step so he could reach the oven. "You can get the garlic bread out of the oven. There are pot holders in the drawer next to the sink."

He laughed. "I don't need pot holders."

"No, I guess you don't." Sometimes I forgot what summer elves were capable of.

He opened the oven, letting out a waft of hot air, then reached in and pulled the foil-wrapped loaf out. "Anything else?"

"That's it." I left the pasta fork in the pot and carried the pot to the table. I put it on the trivet I'd set out earlier, since my table wasn't immune to heat, and filled Cooper's dish first, making sure to give him an extra meaty scoop.

We sat down to eat. The conversation was easy, the food surprisingly tasty, and by the time our bowls were empty, so was my wine glass. I was feeling good. And bad. Because, despite everything I'd promised myself I wouldn't do with Cooper tonight, I really did want to kiss him.

He was so nice, and such a good guy,

and ridiculously hot. Literally and figuratively. Plus, I already knew how much fun kissing him was.

Instead, I got up to clear the table. He grabbed my hand as I reached for his plate. "You've done enough work. Let them sit and I'll take care of them. Later."

His voice was husky, and by the light in his eyes, I knew he was feeling the same thing I was. That old spark. Whatever chemistry we'd had in college hadn't really petered out. Not enough to be forgotten, anyway.

"I have dessert," I said lamely. "Berry tart."

He stood and, still holding my hand, led me to the couch. "Sounds good. But maybe in a few."

He sat and patted the cushion beside him. "C'mon, relax for a minute. We can watch a little TV and just chill. I promise I'll do the dishes in a bit. Only fair since you cooked."

That was sweet. And generous, since my cooking hadn't been much more than heating stuff up. I sat and reached for the remote. I settled on a comedy skit show that might be worth a few laughs. That seemed safe.

When I leaned back, he put his arm around me. "Thanks for dinner."

I glanced at him. His eyes were on the screen. "Thanks for helping me out with the truck this morning."

"Anytime, Jay. Anything for you." He looked at me. "You know that."

My insides did a little flippy-gooey thing. *Snowballs.* This was not good and really good and I was in trouble. And I wasn't sure I cared. I made one more attempt to change the mood we were entering, but all I could do was repeat what I'd said a minute ago. "I have dessert."

"You're all the dessert I need."

Then he leaned in and kissed me, tasting of wine and the sweetness of the tomato sauce. Yes, there was a little garlic in there, but hey, we'd both eaten it. So whatever. It was kissing. And it was good kissing.

Cooper's mouth was soft and warm, and his heat spiraled through me in lazy swells that looped around my bones like a warm summer breeze. Kissing him made me happy. It reminded me of our time together and how amazing that had been.

There was nothing like a first love. And Cooper was mine. *Had* been mine. I reluctantly but firmly broke off contact. "I don't know if we should do this, Coop."

"Why?" His fingers tangled in the ends of my hair. "Because you like the vampire?"

It wasn't news that he knew about Greyson. "I do like him."

"Do you like me too?"

"Yes. But it's more complicated with us."

"Because of our past? If anything, that should make it easier. We know each other. Know how well we get along. How good we are together."

"When we were in college. We're different people now."

He shrugged one shoulder. "Not that different. Sure, we've both matured. You've gotten more beautiful. More confident. And a hell of a lot sexier."

I blushed. How could I not? "I don't exactly feel more confident right now."

He smiled. "I just…I just want to know you haven't counted me out."

My heart melted a little. "I haven't. But are you saying you don't care that I'd be seeing you and Greyson?"

"Do I care? Yes. But you're allowed to like more than one guy. All that matters is which one of us you choose in the end." His expression turned sly and cocky, very much the Cooper I knew from college. "Which I know will be me."

I shook my head. "I know one thing that hasn't changed about you since college."

"What's that?"

"Your ego."

He laughed.

I got up. "I'm getting us some dessert." I headed back to the kitchen.

He leaned back, crossing one long leg over the

other so that his right ankle rested on his left knee. "If opening the box caused Spider to talk, then we need to find out what was in the box."

I nodded as I took the tart out of the fridge. "Already working on that. Birdie Caruthers is trying to get me a visit with Francine Gresham. That's who owns the house. Or did, until it was sold."

He nodded, then paused. "How do you know Birdie? Wait, let me guess. Greyson."

I made a little apologetic shrug. "He's well connected."

"So am I," Cooper said. "When are you going to see Francine?"

I sliced the tart and served it onto two plates, the bigger slice for Coop. "I don't know. Apparently, she's not big on visitors."

He was quiet as I came back with the plates and forks, waiting until I'd put them down on the coffee table to say anything else. "What do you think was in the box?"

"No clue. But there was some faint traces of iridescent green powder inside."

That got me a few more seconds of silence while he leaned over the table and prodded his slice of tart with his fork. "Maybe it was a genie."

"Juniper said the same thing. But how would I know? It's not like I'm an expert on genies. Seems farfetched to me, even in this town. Have you ever met one? I haven't."

Cooper put his fork down. "I have, actually. And I'd be happy to introduce you to her."

"Really? She lives here? When?"

"Right now."

My eyes widened. "For real?"

"Well, I'd have to call her first. See if she's available. But sure."

"It's almost eight thirty."

"She's a night owl." He glanced at his dessert again, but not so fast that I didn't see something in his eyes.

My gaze narrowed. What Cooper had said about us knowing each other was right on. And I knew that look. "How do you know her?"

"We, uh, we dated. A little."

I'd pretty much already figured that out. "I see." I decided to torture him a little. "Just the once, then?"

"Three times, actually. But we didn't have any chemistry."

I nodded sagely. "At least you figured that out before you slept together."

He winced.

I had to bite my tongue to keep from laughing. "I take it you couldn't quite grant her wishes, then?"

His eyes narrowed. "Hah hah."

"You opened the door. I just walked through." I sliced off the end of my tart triangle and forked it up, ready to pop it into my mouth after my next question. "How did you meet her?"

"She's sort of a medical professional. I tweaked my shoulder a while back, and one of the guys at the station recommended her to work on it."

I swallowed my mouthful. "She's a doctor?"

"Not exactly." He sighed. "She's a masseuse."

"Oh, yeah," I said. "That's totally like a medical professional." I rolled my eyes. "Cooper, whatever you did—*whoever* you did—when we weren't together is your business. You don't have to dance around your past. Or your present."

He took a bite of his dessert and swallowed it down. "Yeah, I know, but after everything that happened between us, I don't want anything else to get in the way."

"Then just be honest. The reason we broke up is because we weren't completely honest with each other. Sure, Lark started it with her lies, but if there's any chance for us, we can't hide stuff from each other."

He nodded. "You're right. And I'm sure you've dated lots of guys since we were together. And then there's the vampire." He rolled his eyes.

I snorted. "Please. You think I dated lots of guys in the North Pole? I'm the Winter Princess. Guys willing to date me were either trying to improve their social status or add a notch to their bed post." I fiddled with my fork. "But mostly, they were just intimidated by me. Not many brave souls want to date the woman who will one day rule them."

"I never really thought about that. I suppose that's why you want to keep seeing me and the vampire. To make up for lost time and all that."

"That's part of it." I looked at him, enjoying how pretty he was. "And the other part is that I'm in no rush to settle down. I want to have some fun. And right now, that means dating around."

He nodded. "I understand. The vampire might not, though. Just saying not every guy is as easygoing as I am."

"Greyson's fine with it." At least I thought he was. I guess that was a conversation I needed to have. "Nice try, though. Why don't you call your genie and see if we can swing by her bottle, or whatever she lives in? I'd like to figure out what was in this box."

"Yes, Your Highness." He pulled out his phone.

I made a face at him, then twisted and leaned back on the arm of the couch so I could stick my toes under his thigh.

He cradled the phone between his ear and shoulder so he could scoop my feet into his lap. Where he then proceeded to rub them.

Pretty sure my eyes rolled back in my head. Cooper's hands were big and warm and slightly callused. And the pressure of those hands on my feet was magical. Not sparks in the air magical, but close.

"Hey, Imari, it's Cooper. How are you?" He smiled in a sort of wistful way. Oh, he'd definitely liked her. "Great. No, my shoulder's good, thanks. I was wondering if I could bring a friend by to talk to you. I know it's short notice, but it's a jinn-related emergency. Or might be. Not sure. That's why we need your expert opinion."

His thumbs pressed into the ball of my foot, and I moaned softly, unable to stop myself. His brows lifted, and a look of self-satisfaction came over him. "Half an hour? That would be great. I owe you. Thanks."

He hung up, which required him to take his hands off my tootsies. "She said come on over. Unless you don't want me to stop…"

I didn't. But my cat could talk. Figuring out what had caused that had to come first. I swung my feet off his lap and onto the floor. "Not that that wasn't highly enjoyable, but I think I need to get to the bottom of this box business." I stood. "I'll put the box in a shopping bag and get my purse."

He drove, seeing as how he knew where she lived and I didn't have a car. Turns out, she had an apartment at the Excelsior, the only real condo building in town. It was sleek and modern and not at all like the rest of Nocturne Falls.

I stared up at the building as I got out of the

truck, wrapping the long handles of the shopping bag around my hand. "This place doesn't look like it belongs here."

"Word is it was built specifically for Julian Ellingham. The penthouse apartment is his. And not surprisingly, most of the other residents are women."

I laughed. "So he's a bigger hound dog than you are?"

Coop shot me a look. "You said you didn't care who I dated."

"I don't. I'm just amazed by the sheer volume."

We walked toward the building as he answered me. "Imari is one person."

"So is Toly's granddaughter, and you dated her, which makes two. And she, I might add, tried to kill me."

"Hey, that had nothing to do with me."

"No, but if this chick tries to kill me, I may start thinking differently."

He pulled the lobby door open. "Imari is great, you'll see."

We walked in, and Cooper gave our names to the doorman. "We're here to see Imari Zephara."

Imari Zephara? That was a name and a half.

The doorman nodded. "Yes, Miss Zephara said you'd be arriving." He picked up a house phone and pressed a button, then put it to his ear while speaking to us. "I've called the elevator for you so you can go on up. I'll let her know you're here."

"Thanks." Cooper and I headed for the elevators.

I stayed quiet, just observing. The Excelsior felt like money. Chic and sophisticated and private. The elevator doors slid open with a sigh, the stainless steel exterior giving way to a sleek interior paneled in dark wood and brushed chrome. Cooper touched the button for the second floor, and the doors closed. I knew we were moving, but it was hard to tell.

The whole joint struck me as the kind of place where people lived who wanted to control their interaction with others. Being the Winter Princess, I understood that.

My parents might live in a place like this. Or my aunt and uncle. If any of them ever moved out of the North Pole, which they wouldn't. It wasn't their style aesthetically, but the overall feeling of being protected from the world outside was something that would appeal.

So why did Imari live here? And how much did a massage therapist make in this town? I doubted I'd get the answers to those questions as the doors opened onto a large foyer, also dark wood and brushed chrome, but the wood floor was covered with an expensive-looking Oriental rug, and the walls and reception table held some modern art.

There were three doors marked with sleek numbers and letters.

Cooper knocked on the middle one. 2B.

Or not to be, my mind immediately filled in.

Imari opened the door almost immediately.

I nearly sucked in a breath, but years of court training helped me maintain my composure. I'd seen beautiful women before. But Imari was almost unreal. Big almond eyes, lots of dark wavy hair, full lips, and even in a pair of harem-style lounge pants and a T-shirt, she looked classy.

Next to her, in my shorts and tank top, it was hard not to feel like a big old clump of yellow snow. Even Cooper's light was a little diminished by her.

She smiled at Cooper. "Hello there."

"Hi, Imari. Thanks for letting us come over so late."

She shrugged and glanced at me before answering. "You said it was an emergency. Come on in, and I'll see if I can help."

"Great, thanks. This is Jayne, by the way."

"Hi." I stuck my hand out. "Nice to meet you. Really appreciate any help you can give."

She shook my hand, her touch light, her skin incredibly soft. "Happy to do it."

She ushered us in, and we walked into one of the prettiest apartments I'd ever seen. The walls were painted a deep raspberry, the upholstery was navy and everything else—the rugs, the pillows, the tapestries on the walls—were patterned in every color imaginable. Touches of gold were everywhere. I felt as though I'd stepped into a sultan's lair.

"Your home is so pretty." Made me realize I still had a lot of work to do on my own.

"Thank you. Would you like some tea?"

"No, I'm good, thank you."

Cooper shook his head. "None for me either. We don't want to take up too much of your time."

She gestured toward the couch. "Please sit." She settled on a large ottoman and crossed her legs under her in a yoga pose. "Tell me what I can help you with."

I explained what happened, then took the box out of the shopping bag and handed it to her. "What do you think? Could that have had a genie in it?"

She studied the box briefly, turning it over in her hands. Then she set the lid aside, lifted the box to her face and inhaled. At last, she handed it back to me. "This box never held a genie, but it definitely held something magical."

"Magical how?"

"I'm not sure, but…" She looked at Cooper, then back at me, her brow furrowing. "Whatever was in that box was very powerful." She bit her lip. "And you let it out."

I'd never heard the obvious stated quite so ominously. I glanced at the box. "I did let it out, inadvertently. So what do I do about it? Is this going to be a problem?"

Imari frowned. "It's not a problem exactly, but because you released whatever this magic was, you will have to be the one to put it back in that box."

Fantastic. "Technically, it was my cat who let it out."

"Doesn't matter." She shook her head. "You bought the box. That makes you the owner. The lid was opened while in your possession. There are no technicalities when it comes to this kind of magic."

"This kind?" I needed to know more. A lot more. "Do you have any idea what was in there? Some kind of spell or something maybe? My cat said he could talk because I'd wished for it. And I'm starting to think I had another wish granted.

One about not running out of Dr Pepper. Every time I take one out of the fridge, the six-pack is always full." I tapped my chin. "You know, I could live with that one not being revoked."

"It's jinn-related, whatever it is. Especially if you've had wishes granted." Her gaze narrowed. "If you've truly had two wishes granted, then you should have one more left. You must be very careful what you say from here on out."

"I will be."

Cooper elbowed me. "Good luck with that, Jay."

I glared at him before speaking to Imari again. "How would it normally work if someone had a jinn of some kind they wanted wishes from? I mean, I had wishes granted that I wasn't really making. What if someone was trying to purposefully have wishes granted?"

She tipped her head. "If someone was trying to have wishes granted, they would know what they were dealing with. Typically, they'd start off by addressing the creature to command its attention. Something like, 'My wishes are...' Otherwise, as in your case, the creature will try to escape as soon as possible."

"Which is exactly what it did. But how is it not a genie but jinn-related? I don't get that part."

"Genies are a kind of jinn, but not all jinn are genies. The jinn family includes creatures like pixies, sprites, ghouls. And genies, of course." Imari smiled. "Does that help?"

"Yes, thank you. So I let a creature out of the box. Interesting. I hadn't really thought of it that way. Say, of all the creatures that are jinn, which ones are small enough to fit in that box?"

Imari laughed softly. "All of them."

I looked at her, skeptical. "Even you?"

"Even me."

How about that. Clearly I had a lot to learn about jinn. "Is there any more help you can give me?"

She thought for a moment. "If you could learn the creature's name, you could exert a certain amount of control over it. Hold its attention, get it to listen to you for more than wishes, that sort of thing. But getting its name will be extremely difficult. You'd have to ask it, and without knowing where it is…" She lifted her hands. "Like I said, impossible."

I thought for a moment. "I have one wish left. Can't I use that to get the creature's name?"

"No, that's the one wish it will never grant."

"But you're a genie, right? Can you grant me a wish that I can use to get this magic back in the box? Or find out its name?"

A dark cloud seemed to cover her face. "No. I…no longer do that." She shifted, putting her feet on the floor. "I'm sorry I can't help you, but I suggest you talk to some of the other more knowledgeable supernaturals in town. Magic like this can't be up to any good."

Clearly, my request for a wish hadn't gone over well. Wasn't like I'd meant to upset her. And I still didn't feel like she'd told me everything she knew. "What makes you say that? You're a kind of jinn. You don't seem like you're up to anything nefarious."

Her brows lifted. "What I am and what this creature is are very different. I've never dabbled in this kind of magic, but you must trust me on this. I can tell by the scent it's left behind that there is a darkness in it."

"You can smell darkness? How is that possible?"

"It's like telling the difference between fresh milk and milk about to go off. It's not bad yet, but given enough time, it will be. This creature is very much like that. Make sense?"

"Yes." And more reason than ever for me to see Francine. I stuffed the box and lid back in the shopping bag. "Thank you for the information. Do you think this creature is what caused all the other weird stuff that happened today?"

She frowned. "What other stuff?"

Cooper filled her in about the woman who'd turned blue and the strange calls the fire department had had.

She nodded. "Yes, I definitely do. And while

these things might seem harmless, my guess is, until this magic is contained again, these pranks will grow increasingly more bothersome. And possibly dangerous. That's what I meant about the darkness in it. It's almost like an anger." She got up and glanced toward the door. "That's really all I know."

Cooper touched my shoulder and stood. "Thanks for your help, Imari. We'll see ourselves to the door."

I rose, and he put his hand on my lower back, hustling me straight out and into the elevator, which came pretty quickly. Like it had been summoned. Or maybe it had never left. As soon as the doors closed, he sighed. "I told you not to say anything about wishes."

I turned to him. "It's part of the story, Coop." I shifted the shopping bag to my other hand. "I didn't know it was going to upset her. I just thought you didn't want me asking her because it's like meeting a doctor and asking them straight away what that weird pain in your leg is."

He shook his head. "No, Imari's sensitive about the whole wish thing, which I get is strange for a genie, but it's not a subject she likes to talk about. I don't know why. Like I said, she doesn't elaborate."

"You should have told me that. I wouldn't have said anything." I thought for a moment. "Is that why you guys broke up? Did you ask her for a wish?"

"No. We broke up because…other reasons."

The elevator opened. We walked through the foyer and out to the parking lot. The doorman was signing in a pizza delivery guy but gave us a wave as we went by.

"What other reasons?" I asked as Cooper opened my door to let me into the truck.

He stood there for a moment, sandwiched between me and the door, looking like he was trying to swallow something unpleasant. I could feel the heat radiating off him. Whatever was on his mind was causing him some real emotion.

I shrugged. "If you don't want to tell me—"

"She wasn't you."

My jaw fell open.

He raked a hand through his hair as he looked away for a moment. "It was right after I moved here. I got a little homesick. A little nostalgic. And she was the closest thing to you I could find in this town."

I stared up through my lashes at him, tipping my head down. "In what way is she close to me?"

He leaned his forearm on the cab and met my gaze. "She's beautiful and charming and classy."

All things that seemed completely alien to any description of me right now. In fact, it was like comparing a scoop of vanilla ice cream to a banana

81

split. "Coop, that's sweet, but she's so beyond me that—"

His mouth covered mine in a kiss that was heat and need and yearning. It sent a shiver through me, the cold plunge of feeling like a warning response to his unexpected action. When he pulled away a few seconds later, there were ice crystals on the inside of the windshield.

He sighed and I could see his breath.

I swallowed. Part of my reaction to him was surprise.

And part of it wasn't.

The muscle in his jaw twitched. "Time to take you home."

He shut the door before I could say anything, so I waited until he came around to his side and climbed in. "Coop—"

"You don't need to explain, Jay. I've known you long enough to know that when you freeze up like that, you're unhappy. I shouldn't have kissed you just then. I get it. My bad. Let's move on."

I put my hand on his arm for a second. He was burning up, which meant there was a *lot* going on inside him right now, just like I'm sure my touch felt ice cold. "*Coop*, listen to me. I was a little freaked out by what you said. I mean, comparing me to Imari when she's so clearly on another level? How was I supposed to react? And then you kissed me when I didn't expect you to. It was just a response to the moment, not an indicator of my feelings for you. Which I do not want to discuss, other than to say I like you and I'm glad we're friends again and the kissing is not awful."

He stared at the ceiling of the truck and pursed his mouth. "Just what every guy wants to hear. The kissing isn't awful. At least that's not as bad as 'You're such a nice guy' or 'It's not you, it's me,' because everyone knows it *is* you." He looked at me, his blue eyes as stormy as I'd ever seen them. "And for the record, you are not vanilla. I know Imari's beautiful, but so are you. And you're every bit as classy and amazing as she is. Plus, you're freaking royalty. Give yourself some credit, Jay."

I raised my brows and stared at him. I appreciated his kind words, but he was being driven by emotion right now. Summer elves were prone to that, being so hot-blooded and all. "Are you done?"

He stared right back, peering into me in a way that made me a little squirmy. "I don't know. Am I?"

Are we? That's what he'd meant. "No."

He held my gaze a moment longer. "Okay."

He started the truck and pulled out of the parking lot. We rode in silence until we turned onto Main Street, which was when he spoke again. "Sorry about all that back at the Excelsior. Imari dredged some stuff up in me. But that's out of my system now."

"Don't ever apologize for being real about what you're feeling." His genuineness had always been part of his charm. "That's one of the things I've always loved about you. Still do. There's no guessing where you stand with Cooper Sullivan."

His mouth bent in a little half smile. "I am who I am." He parked in front of the warehouse door and turned to me. "Anything else I can do to help with this box thing?"

I thought a moment. "Let me know if you hear or see any more weird happenings?"

"Will do. I'll get your door." He hopped out and came around to open it for me.

It was sweet and old-fashioned and utterly Cooper. I grabbed my bag and got out, then leaned up and kissed his cheek. "See you soon."

"You know it. Thanks for dinner."

"You're welcome. Night." I headed for the door.

"Night," he called back.

I unlocked the warehouse door, then looked at him right before I went inside. He was leaning on his truck, arms crossed, watching me and smiling this little smile like a kid who'd just gotten away with eating dessert first. His position made the muscles in his shoulders, biceps and forearms pop. The man was very, very pretty.

My insides did a little flippy, fluttery thing. Stupid insides.

I shook my head and went in, smiling anyway because I couldn't help it. Cooper was cocky and sensitive, and that uncommon mix got to me every time. I wanted him around. In my life. As a friend. Or whatever we were that also involved kissing but no firm commitment.

I rode up the elevator and walked to my door. Across the way, I could just make out Juniper's TV playing, and from Buttercup's apartment came the soft thump of an explosion—the soundtrack of one of her video games.

Happiness bubbled up in me, the result of my interesting evening with Coop, my new life here in Nocturne Falls and the friendships I'd made. Just knowing Juniper and Buttercup were across the hall from me was comforting. Sure, I missed my family, but I was making a new one. I pushed the door open and went inside.

And of course, there was Spider. He was curled up on the couch, a tight little ball of black fur with his tail draped over his nose. I went and sat beside him, bending down to kiss his head. "Mama's home, Spidercat."

He yawned and stretched, then curled back up and blinked at me, his green-gold eyes filled with sleepiness. One paw came up to touch my cheek. "Mama," he said. "Spider loves Mama."

Then he tightened into a knot and drifted back to sleep.

I sniffed at the sweetness of his words. "Mama loves you, too, baby."

Maybe having a cat that could talk wasn't so bad after all. I yawned and my bed beckoned, so I gave him another kiss on the head then got to my feet. I left the bag with the box and lid in it on the coffee table. I'd figure out what to do with that in the morning.

I flipped on the bathroom light and went to work scrubbing my face and teeth. Cleaned up and ready for bed, I changed into the new shorty pajamas I'd bought at a boutique in town. They were perfect for the summer heat, cute and made me feel pretty, so I was willing to overlook how much they'd cost. Also, I liked to think I was helping to support the local economy.

I climbed into bed, grabbed my tablet and pulled up the book I was reading. I was a few pages in when Spider hopped up to join me. Of course, he had to sit on my stomach.

I put my tablet down. "Can I help you?"

"Vampire."

I sat up, causing Spider to tumble off. "Greyson?" But what other vampire would it be? "Where?"

Spider walked around me to settle on the pillow my head had just vacated. "Window."

I pointed at him. "Is Greyson really at the window, or did you just do that to get my pillow?"

Spider didn't answer, but the soft rapping on the window in the living room told me all I needed to know.

These cute pajamas were turning out to be an even better investment than I'd imagined. I padded out to the living room.

Yep, Greyson was out there. I raised the window. "You could have called."

He gave my outfit a once-over and smiled. "And miss seeing you in your smalls? I think not." He squinted at the fabric. "Is that…candy?"

I crossed my arms. "Yes, gumdrops and lollipops. What's up?"

"You're not inviting me in?"

"I was in bed."

A dark gleam shone in his eyes. "If you'd rather talk there—"

"You're very cute, but I have an early day tomorrow, and I'm not much closer to figuring out what I let out of that box, so while I'd love to stand here and chat as my AC disappears out the window, maybe you could just kiss me good night and we can talk in the morning."

"I was under the impression you could provide your own magical AC."

"That's beside the point. So can we just chat in the A.M.?"

He slipped in through the window to stand next to me. Some people think cats are super graceful. Those people have never seen Greyson move. "Can't wait until morning."

"No? Why? What's going on?"

He sighed. "There's a bridal shop in town. Ever After. This evening, an hour before closing, all the wedding dresses turned black."

I dropped my arms. "Oh, that's awful."

He nodded. "Corette, the woman who owns the shop, isn't happy. She's a witch, and nothing she's tried has made the dresses right again. Also, she's engaged to Stanhill, the middle Ellingham brother's rook, so this situation just got escalated."

I shrugged. I had no idea what a rook was, but that was beside the point. "I'm still not sure why you're here."

His eyes narrowed. "Because Hugh Ellingham would like to see you."

I pushed my hair off my face. "Fine. Tell him to call my office in the morning, and I'll—"

"No, he'd like to see you *now*."

Realization struck me. "He sent you to bring me back."

Greyson nodded. "Yes."

"How does he know that I might have something to do with the black dresses?"

Greyson pursed his mouth and glanced at the ceiling.

"You told him about me, didn't you?" I put my hands on my hips. "I was in bed."

"I'm sorry." Greyson slipped his hands into my hair, took a step toward me and kissed me. I tried to protest, but just for a second. His mouth was weapons-grade hot.

When I started kissing him back, I felt his mouth curve into a smile and he broke the kiss. "Get some clothes on, lass."

"Kissing me doesn't make this summons any better."

He raised a brow. "Not even a little bit?"

It did. But I wasn't telling him that. I swept away toward the bedroom. "You owe me big-time."

"Duly noted," he called back.

I threw on jeans, a tank top and flip-flops. I wasn't interested in impressing anyone at this hour, and like Cooper had reminded me earlier, I *was* royalty. The Ellinghams might own this town, but my uncle controlled Christmas and my father could arrange for snow to bury the whole town, so these vampires had better remember who they were dealing with. Not that I was inclined to call in those kinds of favors, but I *could*. And that had to count for something. I put on my diamond-stud earrings—a college graduation present from my parents—for good measure.

I grabbed my purse and walked out, picking up

the shopping bag with the box in it on my way past the coffee table. "Are you driving?"

"Happy to, yes."

"All right, let's go." I stepped toward the door as Greyson stepped toward the window. "Whoa. Do you think we're jumping off the fire escape again?"

"I am parked right outside."

I sighed. We'd done that only once, but I hadn't known that's what we'd been about to do either. It had been sort of fun (terrifying, but better once my feet touched ground), but to do it deliberately was something else.

He crooked his finger at me and smiled. "I can make it so you don't notice a thing."

Reluctantly, I walked toward him. "How's that?"

"You'll see." He slipped back onto the fire escape.

I joined him out there and pulled the window shut. It wasn't locked, but I wasn't worried about that. "Okay, what are you going to do?"

He put his arms around me, still grinning like a fool, and pulled me against him so that there was no gap between us. No gap.

Then he kissed me again. I let him. It was the least he could do for interrupting my bedtime. Also, he was a tremendous kisser.

My head went all fizzy, and my stomach followed with a kind of light, floaty feeling.

Then he pulled back. "See?"

"See what?"

He released me to spread his arms wide. "We're not on the fire escape anymore."

I looked around. We were on the sidewalk outside the warehouse door and next to a sleek black muscle car. I hooked my thumb at it. "This yours?"

"Yes." Pride gleamed in his eyes.

"What is it exactly?"

He ran his hand along the side with the same kind of touch I imagined he'd use on a woman. "A 1969 Camaro."

"I suppose now you're going to tell me how it's got four on the floor or a super shifter or some other mechanical thing that I don't understand."

He laughed softly. "I don't know a thing about cars, except that this one is exceptionally good-looking, very fast, and incredibly fun to drive." He strode around to the passenger's side. "Now, if you'd be so kind as to get in. There's another vampire who'd very much like the pleasure of your company."

I can't lie. Hugh Ellingham's house was impressive, but getting to see a magazine-worthy house didn't make up for missing out on sleep. I could be a little cranky when I was tired. In case you hadn't noticed.

At least the ride over had been fun. Greyson hadn't been lying when he'd said his car went fast.

An older, silver-haired gentleman let us in. "Very good, you're here." He nodded at Greyson. "Mr. Garrett."

Greyson nodded back. "Stanhill, this is Jayne Frost. The Winter Princess."

Stanhill sketched a bow, which was unexpected and nice. Although unnecessary.

"Pleased you could join us, Your Highness."

I smirked. "You make it sound like I had a choice. And just Jayne, please."

Greyson made a little noise in his throat that

sounded like a warning. I didn't want to get him in trouble, but I wasn't going to be a wilting flower, either. I had the Frost name to protect, after all.

Stanhill held out his hand toward the house behind him. "Mr. Ellingham is in the library. If you'll just follow me."

And we did, because what choice did we have? But meeting in a library didn't sound so bad. Especially because you were supposed to be quiet in a library. So, you know, no yelling.

The room was impressive. And loaded with books, which was cool, but I was more of an e-book girl myself, now that I was in a place where electronics worked.

The man I assumed to be Hugh Ellingham walked toward us. He was dark-haired and not unattractive, but he was as reserved as Greyson was wild. Even at this late hour, he was in a suit and tie. Or maybe that was because of our meeting. I couldn't be sure.

I already knew he was a vampire, but even if I hadn't, I would have been a little intimidated by him. There was a sense of power about him. And the kind of assurance that came from having had that power for a long time.

My father was the same way. Had the same air about him. But my father was Jack Frost, the Winter King. And as far as I was concerned, this guy was just a vampire with money. I lifted my chin. "You must be Hugh Ellingham."

He smiled and didn't seem nearly as intimidating. "I am. And you must be Princess Jayne."

"Just Jayne, please."

"And you may call me Hugh." He gestured toward one of the long leather couches. "Please sit. Can I get you anything? Coffee? Water?"

"No, I'm fine. Thank you." I sat, and Greyson joined me on the next cushion.

Hugh took the chair closest. "I'm very sorry to disturb you at such a late hour, but we have a situation on our hands."

I nodded. "I heard about the wedding dresses."

Stanhill, who'd taken up a post by the door, snorted. "It looks like a bleedin' funeral in Corette's shop."

I looked at him. "I can imagine."

"Yes," Hugh said. "And you need to fix it."

"Me?" I stared at him, happy I'd left the box in the car. "I'm not responsible for this."

"We know about the incident with the item you purchased at the Greshams' estate sale."

I turned to Greyson. "I suppose you told them."

He had the decency to look apologetic. "Things are happening in town. People want to know why."

"How do you know it's not just this town's general weirdness?"

Hugh cleared his throat. "I don't think so."

"But how do you know? I get that there could be a connection, but I'm not sure how you can *know*."

He glanced at Stanhill. "If you would."

Stanhill nodded. "Right away." He left.

I had no idea what that was about. "All I'm saying is we don't really know what's causing this. And even if it is the box, I have no idea what was in it or how to put it. The most I've been able to find out so far is that it's most likely a jinn-related creature. That's it." I didn't like being on the hook for this. All I'd done was some shopping! And the Greshams were really the ones to blame.

Stanhill returned with a silver tray bearing a corked bottle of dark liquid and a short drinking glass. He set the tray on the table in front of us.

"Thank you," Hugh said.

Stanhill returned to his spot by the door.

Hugh uncorked the bottle and poured some of the dark liquid into the glass. I knew right away what it was. I could tell by the color and the bubbles and the unmistakable smell.

He pushed the glass toward me. "Can you tell me what that is?"

"I can do that without tasting it. But I will." I took a sip. "It's my favorite drink. Dr Pepper. But it's...off somehow. Too sweet. And for me, that's saying something."

Hugh's expression turned smug. "Then I believe we have our proof, Miss Frost."

"How so?"

His smugness disappeared, replaced by a look of sadness. "Because that beverage you just tasted is actually a sample taken from our beautiful falls." He gestured at the bottle. "About the same time Corette's wedding dresses turned black, the water flowing from the mouth of the falls turned into this."

I grimaced. "Are you telling me this Dr Pepper might have had fish in it? Or frogs?" I didn't really want to think about the grossness factor.

"Miss Frost, what I'm telling you is that there is clearly a connection to whatever you released from that box and what is happening in town. Now, any of us could have released this magic just as easily, so it's not as though we're trying to place blame or take punitive measures. This was obviously an unfortunate, supernatural accident. We simply want your help in solving this problem as quickly as possible."

I sighed. "I'd be happy to help. But I don't know anything more about this than you do."

Greyson nudged me. "You could show them the box."

Hugh nodded. "That could be useful."

I glanced at Greyson. "I guess you should give me the keys."

He stood. "No need. I'll fetch the box." He looked at Hugh. "Be right back."

As he left, Hugh smiled tightly. "I am sorry we had to meet this way. I had planned to invite you to a dinner party and welcome you properly, but with my wife being pregnant, things have been a little off schedule lately."

"Did I hear my name?" A pretty woman with an obvious baby bump walked through the door. She approached me, hand out. "Hi, I'm Delaney. You must be Jayne Frost. It's such a pleasure having the Winter Princess in our home."

I stood and shook her hand. "Delaney? As in Delaney's Delectables?"

"That's me." She peered down at the table. "And I can see that neither my husband or Stanhill have bothered to offer you anything *decent*."

"No, they did, but I declined."

She smiled. "But that was probably before you knew what I have in the kitchen."

This was *Delaney*. From Delaney's Delectables. My favorite sweet shop in town. Possibly my favorite sweet shop ever. I wasn't stupid. "And what might that be?"

She started ticking things off on her fingers. "Chocolate-drizzled raspberry crumble bars, mocha marshmallow brownies and butterscotch brown butter blondies." She shrugged. "I've been on a bar cookie binge."

My mouth came open, and my stomach growled in response. "Oh my."

Delaney grinned. "Tell you what. I'll fix you up a little sampler plate, how's that?"

"Sounds perfect." I smiled back, no longer sore about being kept from my beauty sleep. "Thank you. I love your store, by the way. Your stuff is amazing. I buy a big box of goodies every week for the employee break room. And a box for myself," I added a little sheepishly. "Winter elves love sugar."

"Excellent." Delaney's grin widened, and she looked at her husband. "I hope you're being nice to Jayne. We need more winter elves in town."

He nodded as Greyson came back in, bag in hand. "Yes, my love, I'm being nice. I promise."

"Good," she said. Then she turned to me. "I'll be right back with that plate."

"I'll help you, miss," Stanhill said.

She left with Stanhill, and Greyson handed the bag to me. "Here you go."

"Thanks." I took the box and lid out and set them on the table beside the tray of undomesticated Dr Pepper. "This is the box that held whatever's causing this mess."

Hugh reached for it, but asked, "May I?"

"Of course."

He picked it up and turned it over in his hands. "No markings that I can see."

"I didn't find anything written on it either."

He lifted it and gave it a sniff, then wrinkled his nose.

"You smell something?"

He nodded, then took a second, longer sniff. "Magic. But that's as far as my skills can take me. This needs another opinion. From someone far more educated on the subject."

I was about to fill him in on what Imari had told me when Delaney came back with Stanhill. She was carrying a small stack of plates, and he was carrying a large serving platter heaped with goodies that included far more than just the three types of bar cookies she'd described earlier. I saw truffles and fudge and at least three other kinds of regular cookies. Including chocolate chip and sugar.

My little sugar-fueled heart nearly broke with joy. But I reminded myself that the reason I was here wasn't to stuff myself silly. At least not immediately. "I've already shown the box to a woman named Imari. She's a genie. Or was. Not entirely sure what she does now."

"She's a massage therapist at the Nocturne Falls Spa." Delaney put the napkins and small plates on the coffee table, then moved the tray with the bottle of magical Dr Pepper off to the side, making room for the platter of goodies. "I see her once a month for a massage. She's a lovely woman, but I didn't know she's a genie."

Stanhill put the platter down, took a brownie for himself on a napkin and went back to his spot by the door.

I was itching to load one of those little plates up. I didn't. But I wanted to.

Thankfully, Hugh took a plate and put a few cookies on it, breaking the ice. "She keeps pretty quiet about that. Retired genies tend to be very secretive so as not to be hounded for their wishes."

I finally reached for a plate. "I can understand that." One brownie, one blondie, one sugar cookie and two truffles. About a third of what I actually wanted, but a good start. "Anyway, she didn't know what was in the box either, other than a jinn-related creature who could have some naughty tendencies. Do you have someone else in mind that might be able to help?"

Delaney sat on the arm of Hugh's chair. "What about Pandora? Or Corette? Or any of the Williams girls? They're all strong witches."

"True," Hugh said. "But Corette already did her best to return the wedding dresses to their natural state and had no luck. This magic feels beyond their reach."

"Agreed," Greyson said. "Might I have a look at the box?"

Hugh handed it over. "You think it might be something older, don't you?"

Before Greyson answered, he lifted the box to his nose the same as Hugh had done. "I do. Especially if this Imari thinks it's jinn-related."

"Roma?" Hugh asked.

"Could be a Gypsy spell, but it's not one I'm familiar with." Greyson looked up. "It's old. And even if Imari said she didn't know exactly what it was, I agree with her assessment that it's something from the jinn family."

"What makes you think that?" Imari hadn't said, which made me wonder if she'd known more than she'd let on. Maybe she'd thought it would reflect badly on her. Or maybe she just hadn't known.

He rubbed his finger on the inside of the box, then held it up. Iridescent green shimmered on his fingertip like leftover Christmas glitter. "All jinn leave a trace like this behind. Genies, pixies, sprites, imps, ghouls, you name it. It's the residue of their magic."

Hugh blinked. "That's very helpful, Greyson. I had no idea you were so well versed in these types of supernaturals."

"The Roma are very careful when it comes to things in the spirit world."

"I see," Hugh said. "Anything else you can share with us?"

Greyson took a napkin and wiped his finger off, leaving a shiny green streak on the white paper. "Whatever it is, it's young and playful and mischievous. And probably a little angry from being cooped up."

I nodded. "That mostly jives with what Imari said too. How do you know that?"

"The residue is green. If it had been blue or yellow, we probably wouldn't have had a single thing happen in town. But we should be very glad it wasn't red. Red is the worst."

"That's something, then, I guess." But I wasn't feeling very encouraged by his information. Mischievous and angry wasn't good. As we'd already been shown. "How are we going to figure out what this thing is and how to deal with it? Birdie Caruthers is trying to get me an appointment to see Francine Gresham, the woman who originally owned this box, but apparently she's not big on visitors."

Hugh's brows lifted. "Francine Gresham owned this box?"

"Yes. Do you know her?"

His mouth bent like he'd just tasted something sour. "After a fashion. And no, she's not big on visitors." He thought for a moment. "It pains me to say this, but I might know someone who can help. And as much as I hate to be beholden to her for anything, I don't think we have a choice. I can't have Dr Pepper flowing over the falls. We need that water clean and available, or the town runs the risk of being discovered. I have to go to the source."

"No," Delaney said. "You don't mean—"

"I do," Hugh answered. "It's time to bring in Alice Bishop."

"But that means telling your grandmother," Delaney exclaimed.

Hugh snorted. "You think Elenora doesn't already know what's been happening in town?"

"Wait," I said. "Who's Alice Bishop?"

Delaney rolled her eyes. "She's an ancient witch that Hugh's grandmother saved from the Salem gallows. She's incredibly powerful and the woman behind the spell on the falls that makes any human who drinks the water oblivious to the fact that this town is full of supernaturals."

Hugh nodded and sighed. "She's also as deeply in my grandmother's pocket as anyone could be. I love my grandmother dearly, but she can be a bit manipulative at times. And at those times, it's often Alice who carries out her wishes."

"Got it." I took another sugar cookie, having polished off everything else on my plate. "Maybe we should wait and see Francine first. I mean, maybe *you* can get me in to see Francine. Or us. You know what I mean. Anyway, since you know her…"

He frowned. "About that. The Greshams have never been particularly good citizens of Nocturne Falls. Frankly, we weren't unhappy to learn they were selling their house. And Francine only got worse after Roger left."

I leaned forward. I wasn't a gossip, but this was interesting. "How were they not good citizens?"

Hugh's perturbed look increased. "They're both technically human—well, I suppose Roger is borderline. But they're fully aware of the supernatural world around them. And Roger claimed to have some gifts—"

"Psychometry. And Francine reads cards."

"Yes, that's right." Hugh nodded.

I smiled. "Greyson told me."

"Then you also know they had a shop here in town."

"Yes." I snagged a third truffle. "They sold curiosities."

"Not just any curiosities. Those related to the supernatural. And many of those things held real power. They shouldn't have been for sale in an open market like that. They were objects best left to hands that could keep them safe. At the very least, some of the more dangerous items should have been locked away."

He shook his head. "We talked to the Greshams about this on more than one occasion. Offered to buy anything like that that came along. But Roger refused, stating it was his shop and his right to sell whatever he liked. Which it was. Up to a point. And that point was the safety of our town and its population."

"What did you do?"

"We resorted to secret shoppers. We'd have them scout the shop regularly and look for items. When they found something, they had permission to buy it and bring it to us. We were able to secure quite a few rare and risky things this way." He blew out a sharp breath. "Until Roger found out."

I was on the edge of the couch. "Then what happened?"

Hugh's eyes narrowed. "Roger changed his window display to highlight his most recent acquisition. An 1800's antique vampire-hunting kit."

"Son of a nutcracker," I whispered. "What a cold move."

"Indeed," Hugh replied. "Things grew increasingly strained. It seemed Roger went out of his way to stock the most troublesome items he could. We were about to hire counsel when Roger left unexpectedly."

"Another woman," I said.

He nodded. "After that, the shop's demise was a matter of time."

Delaney finished a sugar cookie and wiped the crumbs off her mouth. "What happened to the shop after that?"

I understood Hugh's wry smile, because I already knew the answer to that one. But I let him tell his wife.

He glanced up at her. "A new business moved in."

"Which one?"

His mouth pursed. "Yours."

Eyes rounding, she moved back. "You told me that building was an insurance office."

"It was, but the agency was only there for a month or two before they moved on to a different space."

She punched him playfully in the arm. "Hugh Ellingham, you never said a word about the Greshams' shop being in my space."

"I didn't want you to think the place has bad history. I worried you might not want it if you knew what had been there before."

She snorted. "Fudge balls. I would have taken that shop if it had housed a serial killer support group. Opening my own place was a dream come true."

"Glad to hear that, darling. I assume I'm forgiven, then?"

She put her hand on her well-rounded stomach and smiled. "I suppose. At least for now, until we get this new trouble dealt with. What are we going to do about this loose creature? Do you really trust Alice to help with this?"

He patted her leg. "I'm not sure. On one hand, I do. It's the preservation of the town. On the other hand, if there's any way she can harness this magic for herself, she'll figure out how to do it and store it away for future use."

I shook my head. "I don't think she can. Imari said the way this thing works is I'm the only one who can contain it because I own the box. I'm the one responsible. Sadly."

Greyson put his hand on my arm. "You spent quite a bit of money at that estate sale, didn't you?"

I shrugged. "Depends on your definition of quite a bit, but I dropped some bills. Why?"

"Who took care of the sales?"

"A woman. Bryn something. I got the sense she was brought in by an outside company to take care of the whole thing."

"Can you get in touch with her? Tell her you're interested in a few more things?"

"I think the company's info is on the receipt. Although I don't know if I'll get an answer on a Sunday." Although I thought I knew where Greyson was going with this. "You think I can get Bryn to let me into the house so I can find Francine and talk to her about the box?"

"I do."

"Good idea, Greyson," Hugh said. "If Francine has any idea about what's going on, that might be the only way to get access to her. And I'd like to hold off on involving Alice in this if at all possible."

I stared at the box on the table. "I'll call her first thing in the morning."

But first thing turned out to be more like the three hundredth thing and didn't happen until ten seventeen A.M. My late night had meant I overslept, which turned my morning into a mad rush of getting ready for work. Then there'd been a small issue in the shop when a particularly cranky customer wanted to return two puzzles that hadn't actually come from our shop. Whether or not that was the work of the loose magic, I had no idea, but I finally just caved in the name of customer service and told Juniper to give her a credit. So much for Sundays being more laid-back.

Two Dr Peppers and a stack of chocolate doughnuts later, I was at my desk staring at the receipt from my estate purchase. That's when I noticed that my receipt was twofold. I had a white one and a yellow one. The merchant and customer copies. Odd, but not so unusual.

I dialed the number listed on the receipt and waited for someone to answer.

"Century Estate Sales, Bryn Anderson speaking. How can I help you?"

"Hi, Bryn. I wasn't sure I'd reach you on a Sunday."

"I'm always available. Never know when a client might need me. What can I help you with? Are you interested in using our services?"

"I'm actually calling because I was at one of your sales recently. Don't know if you remember me, but I'm the girl with the blue hair who bought some things at the estate sale in Nocturne Falls yesterday. A painting and a rug and some other—"

"Oh yes! Of course I remember you." She sounded awfully chipper. "I'm so glad you called. I believe I accidentally gave you both copies of the receipt. Really dumb of me. So sorry about that. Do you think we might meet up so that I can get my copy? My boss is a real stickler for accurate records."

"I could put it in the mail to you first thing tomorrow morning. That might be faster if you have to come back to—"

"No, no. I'm still in town. I'd prefer to get it from you in person, if that's all right. In fact, I could swing by your house pretty much anytime."

"Uh, sure, I guess." But I wasn't about to let this unexpected turn of events deter me from getting to the woman who could help me with this box. "Look, the reason I called is I was wondering if there was anything still for sale. I'd love to have another look around the house. Maybe buy a few more things. In fact, we could meet at the house, and I could bring you the receipt then."

She hesitated. Like she was thinking. "The sale is over, but I might be able to make an exception. How's tomorrow morning?"

"I'd have to meet at nine. I have work and—"

"That's perfect. So, uh, are you the one who bought that decorative box?"

Now this was interesting. "Yes. That was among the stuff I bought."

"Excellent! The owner of the estate did *not* mean to sell that piece. In fact, it's my fault the box was on that table to begin with. Anyway, if we could get it back that would be great. It has tremendous sentimental value."

I held back a snort.

"If you could bring that with you tomorrow morning, I'll not only see that you're reimbursed for the purchase price but make sure you get a significant discount on anything else you'd like to buy."

I had a decision to make and I had to make it fast. "I've gotten pretty attached to that box."

Bryn went silent for a moment. When she spoke again, the perkiness was gone, replaced by a more steely tone. "Perhaps we can offer you a slightly higher compensation for it."

"I'm not really interested in money."

"Then what are you interested in?"

I took a breath. "I'd like to speak to Francine Gresham."

More silence. Except for the long, slow intake of breath on Bryn's side. "I'll see what I can do."

"I assume you have my number on your caller ID?"

"Yes, but—"

"Then I'll wait for you to call me back with that assurance before I make any plans for tomorrow."

"You do have the box, don't you?"

"Absolutely."

"You, uh, haven't removed the lid, have you? It's important that we get it back in one piece."

Clearly, Bryn knew the box held something magical. Did she know exactly what? But that was a question best asked in person. I wanted to see her face. "No." That wasn't a lie, because technically, I hadn't removed the lid. Spider had.

"I'll call you back shortly."

"Very good." I hung up.

It took her all of ten minutes to call back. "We're all set. Francine will see you tomorrow morning at nine. Make sure you bring the box."

"And the receipt, right?"

"Uh, yes, the receipt, too."

I smiled at how she'd almost forgotten the supposed importance of that little item. "See you tomorrow." I hung up and went back to work.

But my phone rang again a few minutes later. I didn't recognize the number. "Hello?"

"Princess Jayne? This is Birdie, from the station. You remember me?"

I laughed. "How could I forget you? And Birdie, please just call me Jayne." The princess bit was cute, but really, no one called me that. Unless Cooper or Greyson were teasing me or there was some official North Pole function happening, which obviously, there was not.

"I'll try, but it seems wrong not to call a princess *princess*."

"Until I'm queen, I promise it's not a big deal."

"If you say so. Anyway, I called because I am having a dickens of a time trying to get through to Francine. The woman just doesn't want to be bothered."

I grinned. "Speaking of, what are you doing tomorrow at 9 A.M.?"

"I'm starting my shift at the station at nine. I have to get the coffee going or Hank gets cranky."

"Oh, well, work comes first, I guess." It would have been nice to have a werewolf along. You know, just in case I needed a little backup.

"Why? What's happening tomorrow at nine?"

"I'm meeting with Francine. And I thought you might want to—"

"Hank can make his own coffee. You want to get

some breakfast at Mummy's first? We could meet there at eight."

I hadn't counted on that, but as much as I dreaded getting up even earlier, Birdie seemed like a good friend to have. And her access to the goings-on at the sheriff's department was a real bonus. "Sounds good. Eight A.M. at Mummy's."

"It's a date. How did you get the meeting anyway? I'm impressed."

I relayed the conversation between myself and Bryn.

Birdie hissed. "Ooo, they're a big bunch of hooligans. They know all about that box or they wouldn't want it back. And if it really was just sentimental, they wouldn't care if you'd opened it or not."

"I agree."

"You're not actually going to give her the box, are you?"

I thought about that for a second. "If she knows how to recapture this mischief-making creature, then I might. But I've been told I'm the only one who can do that since I'm the one who let it out."

"Francine won't like that." She clucked her tongue. "But then, she's always been a bit of a sourpuss. You ask me, it's no wonder Roger left her. She always looks like she's been sucking on a lemon, bless her heart."

I stifled a laugh. "Now, you will be on your best behavior tomorrow, won't you?"

"Child, I am the embodiment of genteel civility. Unless you cross me. Then I cannot be held responsible for what happens. But yes, I'll be good."

At least until someone crossed her. But I was a big girl, I could handle a slightly older than middle-aged werewolf. I hoped. "Perfect. See you at Mummy's."

I hung up and dug out the box of eggnog fudge my mother had sent. Just popping the top off filled my office with a smell so sweet and delicious my back teeth started to ache. I grabbed a hunk and took a bite, letting the creamy fudge melt over my tongue. The stuff was like elf crack. I had to share this with Juniper.

I wrapped a piece up in one of the paper napkins I kept in the snack drawer and headed into the shop. I needed to spend a little time on the floor anyway.

Kip was behind the counter with Juniper when I strolled in. The shop wasn't overwhelmed with people, so it was a good chance for him to learn the register. "How's he doing?" I asked her.

"Hey there." She smiled. "He's doing great."

Kip shrugged and grinned shyly. "I have a good teacher."

"Think you can handle the register on your own for a few minutes?"

"No sweat."

"Good. Juni, I need to show you something in the action-figure section." I kept my hands, and the fudge, behind my back.

Her brows knit in curiosity. "Sure thing. Kip, hold down the fort."

"Will do."

She walked with me toward the rear of the store where we stopped in front of an array of superheroes. "What's up?"

"Someone has a little crush on you," I singsonged.

"What? Kip? No way."

"Uh, yes. Did you see the way he looks at you?"

"Well, he can crush all he wants. I'm with Pete." She crossed her arms. "What did you want to show me?"

I put my hand in front of me, the paper towel-wrapped treat front and center. "This."

She sucked in a breath. "I smell something sweet. And it smells like eggnog."

I pulled the paper towel back. "It's my aunt's eggnog fudge. It's kinda famous."

Juniper let out a soft squeal. "Are you snowing me? Your aunt. As in Martha Kringle. Santa's wife. This is *her* eggnog fudge?"

"Yep." I laughed. "Are you going to take it or let it melt in my hand?"

She snatched it up and took a bite. A second

later, she groaned and closed her eyes. "Oh wow, that is unbelievable." She looked at me. "Please tell me you can get more of this."

"I do know the woman who makes it."

Kip came skidding around the corner. "Miss Frost? I'm sorry to interrupt, but there's a man at the counter who says he needs to speak to you immediately."

I started walking. "Upset customer?"

Kip shook his head. "I don't think so…"

Cooper stood by the counter, hands on his hips and a scowl on his face. It was a hot look, especially when you threw in the effect of him in his fireman uniform. Plus, there was something about Cooper angry that made him even prettier. "We need to talk. Now."

"In my office," I responded. I had no idea what he wanted to talk about, but discussing my personal business in front of my employees or my customers wasn't going to happen. I didn't wait for Cooper to respond, just spun on my heel and stalked toward the warehouse door.

The thump of his lug-soled work boots on the store's polished concrete floors told me he'd followed. Then a second or two after the warehouse door shut, he grabbed my arm and turned me around.

"I get not wanting to talk in the store, but this is far enough. You've got to figure out how to stop this magic and now."

He was certainly worked up. "What happened? More cats in trees?"

"No." His blue eyes clouded with frustration. "But you're not far off. Engine number one is on top of the fire station. And no one knows how it got there. Except we do."

Snowballs. "On top of the building?"

"Yes. And this isn't funny anymore. You need to do something about this and fast."

"I never thought it was funny, and if I could have done something by now, I would have."

He took a breath. "Sorry. I didn't mean to imply you were just letting this happen. I know you're not. But it's been a very stressful day."

"I can imagine. I'm really sorry about your fire truck. Please tell me the town has another one in case there's actually a fire before we can get number one down."

"We do." He let out a hard exhale and popped his jaw from side to side. "It feels like these pranks are getting worse."

"To me, too. But first thing tomorrow I'm meeting with Francine, so I'm hoping she can shed some light on what this magic is specifically and how to stop it."

That seemed to relax him. "Good." He rubbed the back of his neck. "I'm sorry about the outburst."

I shrugged. "I get it. Stress happens." And he was clearly stressed based on the little shimmers of heat coming off him.

"Yeah, but I shouldn't take it out on you." He shook his head.

I felt for him. "I bet your chief had a few words to say."

Cooper snorted. "Boy, did he."

My phone rang. "Hold that thought." I pulled it out of my back pocket and checked the screen. It was Greyson. I answered. "Hey, can I call you back?"

"No. We have a problem."

I had a pretty good idea I knew what that was. "Is this about the fire truck on top of the station?"

He hesitated. "How did you—the all-American elf is there, isn't he?"

I shifted a little so Cooper couldn't see my smile. "Yes, and I'll call you later."

"Tell me I can take you to dinner tonight and you won't have to call me later."

I twirled a length of hair around one finger and decided to make him work for it. "I have an early morning."

"I could come over. With Salvatore's."

Which was only the best pizza on earth. Clearly, the man knew my weaknesses. "Sold." So much for making him work for it.

"Seven?"

"Perfect."

"See you then, Princess."

With a smirk, I hung up. "Sorry about that. This whole magic-gone-wrong thing has made me a lot more popular."

"I'm sure. Listen, about what I was saying. I really am sorry for taking my stress out on you. How about you let me make it up to you with dinner at Howler's tonight?"

I bit my lip. Greyson's timing was impeccable. "I can't tonight. I'm having breakfast with Birdie Caruthers at eight A.M. tomorrow—she's going with me to Francine's—and besides, I already have plans. Another time, though."

He rolled his eyes. And it sort of seemed like he flexed a little. Like he was trying to show me what I was missing. "Let me guess. You're going out with the undead leprechaun."

"Coop." I shot him a look. "Greyson and I aren't technically going out. He's…coming over. Just like you did last night."

"Touché." He held his hands up. "Well, I'm not going to tell you to have fun."

"Understood." I turned my phone over in my hands. "I should probably get back to work."

"Me too. The chief will be wondering what happened to me." He leaned in and kissed me, nothing major, just a soft brush of his lips on mine and enough to raise my pulse a few beats. "See you later, beautiful."

I swallowed and waved. "Bye."

He went back through the shop door, and I returned to my office, where I immediately finished the hunk of eggnog fudge sitting on my desk. Men were awesome and confusing, and I was never going to be able to decide between Cooper and Greyson.

Unless one of them gave me an ultimatum, which I really hoped didn't happen. I didn't want to be forced to make a choice, and honestly, if one of them insisted I choose, I was probably not going to pick him.

But that wasn't happening today, and by five, I was ready to head up to my apartment and spend some quality time doing nothing with my talking cat. At least until Greyson came over with the best pizza ever.

I went into the shop to say hi to Buttercup and Holly as they took over for Kip and Juniper. The store was busy with the pre-dinner crowd. "How was the day, Juni?"

"Good." She waved a hand at the sales floor. "And still going strong as you can see. How was your day? Everything all right with Cooper?"

"It will be as soon as I figure out how to deal with that wayward magic." I turned to Holly, ready to change the subject. "How are you getting on?"

"Great. Thank you. I love working here."

"Glad to hear it." She'd arrived a few days after Kip but seemed to be catching on.

Buttercup came out from the back of the store. "Hey, Jayne. How's it going?"

"Good, you?"

"Can't complain." She smirked. "And if I could you would have heard about it already."

I laughed. "I'm sure."

"Thanks for the promotion, by the way."

"You earned it."

Juniper and Kip took their aprons off, and we all walked to the elevator. I pushed the up button, but Kip backed toward the warehouse door.

"I'm headed to Howler's for happy hour. You guys want to join me?"

"Another time maybe," I said. "I have a date."

"So do I." Juniper gave him a wave. "But you have fun."

He gave us a salute and was gone.

I watched him go. "He seems to be working out pretty—"

Juniper spun around. "Cooper or Greyson?"

"Greyson." The elevator door opened, and we got on.

She pursed her lips in a rather judgmental way as she pushed the button for the second floor.

"Hey," I said. "You ought to like him. Or at least give him some credit. He's the only one so far who's been able to give me any clue about what was in that box. But I hope to find out more tomorrow." I told her about my impending meeting with Francine and taking Birdie along.

"That sounds promising. How was dinner with Cooper last night?"

"Good. And before you ask, yes, there was kissing, but that's all I'm saying about that."

She shook her head. "I told you so."

The elevator chimed that we'd arrived, and we got off on our floor. I fished my keys out. "You and Pete going out?"

"Staying in. He's bringing Thai. We're going to watch last night's King of the Kitchen episode. I DVR'd it. What about you guys?"

"Greyson's bringing Salvatore's, and then we're going to make out like teenagers." Maybe. Maybe not.

She rolled her eyes. "Keep the moaning to a minimum, will you?"

I laughed as I turned the key and pushed the door open. "You too. Pete looks like he has the potential to get handsy."

She stuck her tongue out at me, then waved and disappeared into her place.

I closed the door behind me. "Spider, Mama's home. You hungry?"

He came zipping out from the bedroom and slid halfway through the living room until he hit the edge of the new rug and tumbled over once. He popped back up to meow. "Yesssss. Starving. Dying. Mama was gone forever."

"Wow. Okay, chill. I'm here now. And I leave

every day, but I'm always coming back. I promise." I scooped him up and kissed his head. "Dinner is on its way."

I carried him over to his dish and put him down, then got to work fixing him a bowl of Chicken Party, his newest addiction. He wound around my legs, purring. Except when I listened closer, he was actually saying, "Hurry, hurry, hurry."

I put the dish down and watched him dig in. "Don't forget to breathe."

He was too busy eating to answer me. I went to freshen up and change into something more comfortable. Not that my sundress wasn't comfortable, but work clothes weren't lie-around-the-house clothes. And since I hadn't dressed up for Cooper, I wasn't dressing up for Greyson either. Black yoga pants and a tank top was as much effort as I was making.

Once in my new outfit, I pulled my hair into a high ponytail and went back out to the living room. Spider was sitting on the window sill, cleaning his face.

"How was dinner, baby?"

He looked up. "Spider loves Chicken Party."

I nodded. "You sure do." I grabbed a Dr Pepper and shut the fridge. Then, out of curiosity, I opened the fridge again. The space where I'd taken the bottle from was already filled. Yep, just as I'd suspected. The supply was never ending. "Weird. But cool."

Whatever. I wasn't going to complain about that. Then I tried to imagine what the falls must look like with all that Dr Pepper spilling over them. Was it weird that I kind of wanted to swim in it? Would I be able to absorb the sugar and caffeine through my skin? Because that could be interesting. Or maybe I was overthinking this. I went to the couch, settled in, turned the TV on low and gave the snow globe a shake.

My dad showed up a few seconds later. "Hey, Jay. How are you, honey?"

"Good. How are you? Everything chill?"

"Everything's very chill. Did the box come through the Santa's Bag all right?"

"It sure did. That's why I'm calling. I want to thank Mom for her care package."

He smiled. "Hang on, I'll get her."

He disappeared for a minute, and I could hear him calling for her. "Jayne's on the globe. Yes, right now."

She popped up right after that, waving. "Hi, honey. How are you? Are you doing all right? Are you eating? Did you get my package? Your aunt sent something too. Do you need anything? I can be there in a couple days if you need me."

I laughed to myself. That was my mom. "I'm good and I got everything you and Aunt Martha sent. And as much as I'd love to see you, there's no pressing need." I really preferred that she didn't visit until this craziness was over. "I had some of the cookies and the fudge today. I gave a piece of the fudge to one of my friends. She's an employee, and she went crazy for it. You and Aunt Martha are going to have to send me a box at least once a month."

She beamed. "We'd be happy to. What's your friend's name, dear?"

"Juniper. She's the dayshift manager. You'd love her."

"I'm sure I would. I'm glad you've made a friend."

"More than one." But I wasn't about to tell her about Cooper. Not yet. Plus, it would take me too long to explain why I was once again dating the guy who broke my heart in college.

"You like it there?"

"I do. Very much. Hey, you want to see how I'm fixing up the apartment?"

"Yes, absolutely."

I carried the snow globe around, showing her the painting and the rug I'd bought. Then I shifted it so she could see Spider, who was now cleaning his back leg. "And that's my cat, Spider."

Who I really hoped didn't say anything right now. I didn't want to explain that either. I tried to get Spider's attention. "He's become quite, uh, vocal lately, but fortunately he hasn't learned English yet." I hoped he got the hint.

"Oh, he's so cute," my mom said. "What a sweet little baby. I'm glad you have company."

I looked into the globe again. "Thanks, Mom. Anyway, that's about it. I really appreciate the stuff you sent. Tell Aunt Martha I said thanks, too, okay?"

"I will, honey. You take care of yourself. Love you."

"Love you too."

The snow settled, and her face disappeared.

I put the globe back on the side table and settled in to watch a little TV until Greyson arrived. Spider came over and sat next to me, putting his front paws on my leg.

He looked up at me. "Your mama thinks Spider is cute."

I scratched his head and smiled at him. "Everyone thinks you're cute. Because you are."

He started purring and shoved his head harder against my fingers. A few minutes later, his eyes were closed and he was curled up next to me asleep. We stayed like that until Greyson knocked on my door.

Which was ten minutes after seven. Greyson wasn't always early like Cooper, but he wasn't the kind of guy to show up significantly late either.

The look on his face said something was up. I took the pizza out of his hands as he came in. "What's going on? More magical mayhem?"

127

"Yes. All the signs on Main Street have had their letters reversed." He sighed and gave me a look. "Except on Santa's Workshop."

Snowballs. "Great. So I'm under some kind of protection because I'm the one who let it loose?"

"Apparently." He leaned on the kitchen counter while I got plates out. "Hugh Ellingham released a statement saying it was the result of a young witch's spell gone wrong and would be corrected as soon as possible."

"Great, one more thing for the witches to get mad about. Like the black wedding dresses weren't enough."

"Actually, the story was Corette's idea."

"Really? Wow. Nice of her to cover for me. And nice of Hugh to put it out there."

"Agreed. But despite those efforts, people in town are starting to talk. They're not idiots. Most of them have lived here long enough to know when something's planned and when something's not."

"Starting to talk?" I snorted as I opened the pizza box. "You'd think they'd be neck-deep in discussions about this by now."

"I mean about you. Word is out that you're responsible for freeing this magic, and now with your shop not being affected…people aren't happy."

I was losing my appetite. A little. I put slices on both plates. "I'm sure they aren't, but I can't help it.

I'm going to see Francine tomorrow. I don't know what else to do, but I'm open to suggestions. Do you have any?"

He nodded. "Go see her tonight."

I closed the pizza box and handed him a plate. "If only I could."

His expression darkened a bit. He took the plate and set it on the counter. "You can if you want to. I can make it happen."

"Greyson, getting an appointment with her took some serious finagling. If you're telling me you can just call her and it's a done deal, then why didn't you offer to do that sooner?"

"I'm not talking about calling her." The muscles in his jaw tightened, and the light in his eyes took on a hard, metallic gleam. I'd seen that light before, but not combined with this dark demeanor. "I'm talking about going over there and demanding she explain this mess. And using whatever means necessary to make that happen."

"I'm not that kind of elf."

"Maybe not, but I can be that kind of vampire."

"I don't know. That sounds dangerous. We don't know what Francine is capable of. What other magic objects or devices she might have up her sleeve."

"No, we don't." The hard line of his mouth relaxed. "But I'll be there to protect you."

I studied him a moment while I thought about

all the nonsense my little purchase had caused. I did not want a reputation in this town as a troublemaker. It could ruin the shop's business. Plus, I was the Winter Princess. Someday I was going to have an entire kingdom to safeguard. There was no better time to practice those skills than now.

"I'd better change."

"We'll go after we eat." He opened the pizza box. "Some things are better done under the cover of darkness. Even in this town."

The Greshams' old Victorian looked a lot different at night than it had yesterday morning. For one thing, it had gone from slightly creepy to full-on eerie, and for another, its potential to be a haunted mansion seemed more like a probability now.

I stared at the house from the safe interior of Greyson's Camaro. "I think it's only fair to tell you that this is freaking me out a little. The house looks...menacing. That's really the only word I can come up with."

He laughed.

I looked at him. "You think my fear is funny?"

"Not at all. But it amuses me that a house can scare you when you're sitting next to a vampire, one of the most dangerous of all the supernaturals."

I squinted at him. "If this was all some elaborate

plot to turn me into your dinner, I'd like to remind you that an ice dagger leaves no trace when it melts. So you're also sitting next to a very dangerous supernatural. Just saying." For added emphasis, I lowered the temperature in the car by about thirty degrees.

He shivered. Probably more for show than anything. I didn't get the sense that vampires were much affected by temperature. Unless they were frozen solid. Hmm. Come to think of it, he might not have been acting considering what had happened a few months ago when he actually had been frozen solid. He put his hand on the door handle. "Point taken. But this needs to be done."

We got out of the car and walked up the long drive to the front door, the deep shadows of twilight fast turning into the full black of evening. I hugged the shopping bag to my side. There were a few lights on in the house, but the curtains were drawn, and the place was silent. No television, no radio, no music, no tortured wailing from anyone being held captive. Just saying.

He knocked. We waited. Nothing.

Then the lights went out.

He grunted. "I guess we're doing this the hard way."

I put my hand on his arm. "You're not going to hurt her, are you? She *is* an older woman living alone. And we're knocking on her door after dark. I'd be wary too."

"I'm not going to hurt her." He frowned. "But we need some answers. I'll be as nice as I can." He leaned in and kissed me, a fast little peck of reassurance. "Be right back."

And then he was gone in a blur of movement that was barely discernible in the dark. I stood there, waiting, looking around for any neighbors who might be watching. I didn't see any. I heard some soft noises. A faint rapping sound, the scrap of a window sash, quiet voices. Then silence.

Which was finally broken by footsteps and the door opening.

Francine Gresham stared out at me, a thin woman with a pinched face and a permanent frown. Greyson stood deeper in the foyer, his gaze on Francine. She looked me over, then sighed. "Come in."

It was about as cheerful a greeting as one might expect from a woman in a nightgown with a scowl on her face and a vampire at her back. I tried to smooth things over. "I really appreciate—"

"Save the small talk," she snapped as she turned around.

I raised my brows but followed her as she swanned past Greyson. She led us into the kitchen. It was one of the few rooms in the house that still had furniture in use. At least on this floor.

She faced us, but her gaze was on the shopping bag hanging off my shoulder. "I understand you have my box."

I was dying to know how Greyson had gotten us in, but that would have to wait. "I bought a box from your estate sale, yes."

"Bryn told me you'd be bringing it tomorrow morning, so I expect you brought it tonight. If not, this conversation is over." She glared at Greyson. "No matter what you think you're owed."

"She has the box," he answered. "But we want answers first."

Hard to believe Francine's frown could deepen, but it did. "What kind of answers?"

Greyson moved closer to me. "What's in the box?"

"A little magic. Nothing for you to be concerned with. Now hand it over."

Greyson didn't give up that easily. "What kind of magic?"

A moment of silence was followed by a long sigh of exasperation. "I don't know. I bought it sight unseen with only the promise that it held something of reasonable power. That happens in my business sometimes."

"Your business?" I asked. "I thought the shop was closed."

"It is. But I still have clients that I acquire for. It's enough of a business for me." She lifted her chin.

"More than I need, actually. And it will allow me to leave this house and this dreadful town behind and start a new life."

"So you don't know what's in the box?"

She shrugged at me. "I only know it's what my client wanted and I brokered the deal. Bryn put the box out for sale not realizing what it was. Then she lost your receipt and we couldn't find you, so you bringing the box to me is appreciated. That's the only reason I'm willing to share as much as I have."

Greyson gave me a short nod. I opened the tote bag and pulled the box out, gripping it in my hands. I'd stuck the lid back on as tightly as possible on the way over. I wasn't sure it would pass as being unopened, but it also didn't matter. At some point we were going to have to get around to the fact that the lid had come off.

Greyson crossed his arms. "You're lying. You know more."

Francine huffed. "How dare you come into my house and accuse me—"

"What's in the box, Francine?" Greyson tipped his head toward it. "Or should we just open it now and—"

"No!" She lifted her hands. "You can't let it out or…"

"Or what?" he asked.

She sighed and stared out the back window for a

moment before facing us again with a brand new scowl. "Just give me my damn box."

Greyson shook his head slowly. "It's not yours anymore and it's already been opened."

Her jaw practically unhinged and she blinked in disbelief. Then she started forward, her hands clenched into fists. "You stupid girl."

Greyson snarled and stepped in front of me, his posture defensive. "Don't take another step toward her, Francine, and don't talk to Jayne that way."

Francine's lid looked like it was about to come loose. "She doesn't know what she's done. What she's set free."

"Then tell her." Greyson's voice held a gravelly command.

"That is why we're here," I said over his shoulder. "And I didn't open it on purpose. My cat knocked it off a table."

She took a step back, but the squall in her eyes remained.

Greyson relaxed a little, moving to stand beside me again.

Francine twisted her hands together. "There was an imp in the box."

"I knew it," he muttered. "What kind?"

"A chaos imp. At least, that's what I paid for."

I glanced at the box in my hands. "That explains what's going on in town. How do I get it back in the box?"

Francine's laugh screeched out of her with no real humor attached to it. "I have no earthly idea. That wasn't my responsibility. I've told you all I know." She glared at Greyson. "Satisfied?"

"Not hardly. Why don't you tell us who the client was? And how we can get in touch with them?"

Francine lifted her chin. "I don't release my client information. Now I would like to go to bed."

I huffed out a breath. "I guess that will do. For now."

Her eyes narrowed. "Not for now. For good. I don't know anything else. Except that it's time for you to leave."

I was frustrated, but further conversation with Francine felt pointless. I stuck the box back in the tote bag as Greyson and I left.

We got back in his car and headed for my apartment. He was almost simmering beside me.

So I stated the obvious. "You're not happy."

"She's lying about something."

"You think she knows how to get the imp back in the box?"

He shook his head. "No. I think she's telling the truth about that. But there's more to this. I can feel it."

"How did you get her to let us in?"

He sat back, his shoulders dropping. A little smirk played across his mouth. "I told her that if she didn't let us in tonight, I'd tell the Ellinghams that she was dealing in relics."

"Relics?"

He made a face. "The bones and teeth of supernaturals. They demand a high price in certain circles. Namely, those that practice the darker magics."

"Like the people who use the underweb?" I'd learned about that particular dark corner of the Internet when the shop employees had gone missing.

"Exactly. I wouldn't be surprised if the underweb is how she finds most of her clients."

I grimaced. "I don't really want to know any more about that."

He laughed. "That's the right response." He turned onto my street. "I'm sorry we couldn't find out more from her."

"We know what was in the box now, though. That's kind of a big thing. With that info, we should be able to figure out what it will take to get it back in. But…" I thought for a second as he parked outside the warehouse.

"What?"

"This chaos imp strikes me as a pretty specialized sort of magic."

"It is."

"And that kind of highly specialized magic would be very expensive, wouldn't it?"

He turned toward me. "Very. I would think."

"So whoever was buying this imp from Francine probably paid a lot of money for it. Money he or she is going to expect to be returned if no imp is produced."

He nodded. "Francine's going to have to come up with that imp or return the money, and judging by the paperwork I saw on the kitchen counter, she's already spent it."

"What paperwork?"

"A copy of a real estate contract for a condo in North Carolina."

"Wow." I slumped in the seat. "This could get ugly."

"Uglier, you mean. And yes, it could. But you let me worry about Francine. I'll tell the Ellinghams what we've found out and they can help us keep an eye on her. All you need to do is find out how to get that thing back in the box and this town put right again."

"Oh well, if that's all." I rolled my eyes. "If it's okay with you, I'm going to bed. It's been an interesting evening, but I still have breakfast with Birdie first thing tomorrow. Although I guess I could text her that our meeting is off."

"No, go to breakfast. Let Birdie in on what you've found out too. Then put her to work to find someone who can tell you how to recapture an imp."

"Okay. Thanks for the pizza. I guess I'll see you later?"

He took my hand and pressed a kiss to my knuckles. "I'll let you know the minute I find out anything new. And you do the same."

"I will."

"Good. And then when this is all over, we'll have a proper night out at Claude's. What do you say?"

"I say that sounds great."

He leaned in and kissed me, soft and sweet and a little apologetic. Maybe because our evening hadn't gone as planned. But being responsible for a chaos imp running rampant in town had to take precedence.

I got out, made my way up to my apartment and crashed, exhausted by the night's activities.

I woke up to Spider sitting on me, tapping my face with his paw. "Mama, Spider hungry. Hungry, Mama. *Hungry.*"

"Dude. It's Monday morning. Have a little sympathy." I squinted up at him, the morning light coming in through the blinds making it impossible to ignore that it was probably time to get up anyway. I peeked at the clock. A little after seven. I groaned. "Okay, fine. Breakfast is coming."

With a happy little meow, he jumped onto the floor and scampered toward the kitchen. I followed, decidedly not scampering. More like the shuffle of the undead. Which made me think about Greyson and smile.

Not that he shuffled.

I fixed Spider a dish of food, more Chicken Party, and put it down in front of him, then helped myself to a Dr Pepper and a cold slice of pizza. Yes, I was going out for breakfast at Mummy's, but last night's dinner had been skimpy on account of us rushing off to see Francine, so I needed a little something in my system or I might pass out from low blood sugar while I was in the shower. What? It could happen.

I checked my phone for messages while I chewed and listened to Spider's happy eating noises. I had a bunch of texts.

First, two from Cooper telling me Engine Number One had been levitated down off the building thanks to the local coven and could we do dinner.

I wasn't thinking clearly enough to figure out my schedule at the moment so I went on to the next message. It was from Birdie, reminding me about breakfast. It was like she knew I was eating leftovers. I gave that message a little side-eye and moved on to the next one.

And almost dropped my Dr Pepper. It was from Lark. My former best friend. The woman who'd single-handedly broken Cooper and me up so she could make a play for him herself.

I stared at the message, the cold pizza growing colder in my mouth. I swallowed the bite of cheese and dough without tasting it. I was trembling slightly from the blizzard of emotions running through me. That text required a reread.

I heard you're in the states now. Hope everything is chill.

I didn't know what to do with that. Did she expect an answer? Did she think we could just pick up after years of not talking? Did she have any idea I knew what she'd done? Had Cooper talked to her? Chill? For real?

I wasn't in the right head space to figure any of it out. Lark would have to wait. And dinner with Cooper seemed like a good idea. At the very least, I could get his take on her message.

I sent him a quick text saying dinner at seven would be great. I left Lark out of it. No point in bringing that up until I had to.

I put my phone back on the counter and stared at it, trying not to think about Lark and the trouble she'd caused and failing.

This wasn't the way I'd imagined I'd be starting my day, but on the plus side, I was definitely awake now.

I knew I liked Birdie, but after she placed her breakfast order, I realized she might actually be my spirit animal. Hey, it was possible. She was a werewolf, after all.

Admiration continued to overwhelm me as our server walked away to put our order into the kitchen. I had to say something. "Blueberry pancakes, a side of bacon, a cinnamon roll *and* a cheese omelet?"

Birdie adjusted her napkin on her lap in a very ladylike manner, her mouth fixed in a prim little smile. "Well, I need my protein."

Sure, because the cheese omelet was what put that order over the top. And all I'd gotten was strawberry cheesecake-stuffed French toast and sausage links. "You're kind of amazing."

She smiled and leaned in conspiratorially, although our back booth was pretty private. "You know how it is. We supernaturals have very high metabolisms. And I did go for quite a run last night."

The thought of Birdie in her wolf form was incredibly intriguing, but we had business to discuss. "Speaking of yesterday, I have some news."

I filled her in on what Greyson and I had done last night, what we'd found out and how she and I didn't need to go see Francine this morning because of it.

"At least we know what we're dealing with now." Birdie's eyes tapered down. "Sounds like she's hiding something."

"That's what Greyson said too."

Birdie shook her finger. "Mark my words, that woman is an odd duck."

I straightened my silverware. "She wasn't thrilled to see us."

"I'm sure she wasn't."

"Greyson had to *encourage* her to get her to let us in."

Birdie rolled her lips in like she was suppressing a laugh. "I'm sure he did."

There was a break in the conversation while our server brought our drinks. Ice water for me and a cappuccino for Birdie. I squeezed the lemon wedge on the side of the glass into my water. "Now that I've met Francine, I totally see what you mean about her looking sour."

"Doesn't she have a puss on her? My word, the woman could curdle milk just by being in the same room with it." She waved her hand. "But never mind that. We have work to do. A puzzle to figure out. Namely, how to get that imp back in that box."

"Right."

She lifted her cappuccino for a sip, then set it back down. "We need to talk to the experts in town. The witches. We should start with Corette, I think. She's a wealth of knowledge and the secretary of the local coven. Plus, she's one of the most accessible of the older witches."

"Is she the one who owns the bridal shop? I don't think she's going to be all that willing to speak to me after what happened to her dresses."

"Corette? Oh, she's not the kind to hold a grudge, and she's certainly not going to blame you for something that was an accident. She might be upset about her store looking like a funeral gathering, but she'll help if it's going to result in all of this getting fixed."

"Good to know. Should we go see her after breakfast? I have time now that we're not going to Francine's."

"Do you have the box? It would probably help if she could examine it in person."

"It's in my apartment, which is only five minutes away."

Birdie nodded and pulled out her phone. "I'll

text her right now and set it up if she's available." Our food arrived as Birdie was finishing up. "We're good to go. She'll meet us at her shop in an hour. I hope that's enough time for us to eat."

The array of food before us was impressive. "It should be plenty." The sweet, strawberry scent of the French toast made my mouth water. I picked up the little jug of syrup. "I can't imagine anything on this table's going to last that long anyway."

Birdie held up a forkful of blueberry pancakes. "That's the spirit."

Twenty minutes later, there were no survivors. Between Birdie and I, we'd cleaned our plates, barely leaving a hint of syrup or a stray berry behind. I insisted on paying the check, although Birdie protested. It only seemed fair since she was here to help me.

We had time to kill, but that was fine since I needed to retrieve the box from my apartment.

Birdie walked with me, happy to go along. "I love Santa's Workshop. I buy all my grandnephew's presents there. Charlie loves video games."

"Does he? We sometimes get toys in the shop that aren't available anywhere else. Sort of testing the waters, as it were. If any video games come in like that, I'll let you know."

"He'd love that, thank you."

I let us into the building. We went up the elevator and down the hall to my apartment. "I should warn you before we go in. Thanks to the imp, my cat can talk and I never know what he's going to say." Although he'd yet to talk in front of anyone but me.

"No worries." Birdie adjusted the straps of her big floral handbag. "I'm sure people say the same thing about me."

I snorted as I unlocked the door. "I'm going to leave that one alone." I pushed it open. "Spider, it's me. And I have a visitor."

He trotted out from the bedroom. Judging by his sleepy eyes, we'd woken him up. He looked at me, then at Birdie.

He stopped dead in his tracks, his eyes going wide. A low growl came out of him, then he hissed and arched his back and his tail puffed up like a bottle brush.

I glared at him. "Spider, what's wrong with you?"

He meowed and ran back into the bedroom.

"What on earth…" I glanced at Birdie. "Sorry about that. He's never done that before, I swear."

She shrugged good-naturedly. "Honey, I'm a werewolf. I'd be surprised if he *didn't* have a reaction to me."

"Well, maybe. But it still seems rude." The box was on the kitchen table where I'd left it last night, still in its tote bag. I grabbed it, and we were on our way.

The walk to Corette's bridal shop got us there a few minutes before nine. It was a cute store. What I could see of it. The words Closed for Restocking had been painted on the paper covering the display windows. I felt bad. That lie was my doing. Inadvertent, but still my doing. Despite what Birdie had said about Corette, I couldn't help but feel that the woman would blame me a little.

Birdie knocked on the glass door, then turned to me and said, "Don't."

"Don't what?"

"Do what you're doing. What you're thinking. You're making yourself feel bad about this, and it's not your fault. Letting that imp out wasn't purposeful. It was an accident."

"I know, but—"

"No," she said firmly. "It's fine to be sorry but another to let the guilt be a millstone about your pretty neck." She gave me a very motherly look. "Things happen. More so in this town."

The door opened to reveal a lovely older woman in a trim periwinkle suit and pearls. "Birdie, Miss Frost. Do come in."

The shop's interior was just as I'd imagined a bridal shop should look. Pretty pastels, crystal chandeliers and soft lighting. The black dresses were so out of place it almost hurt to look at them. Like a shiner on a beauty queen.

I sighed as Corette locked the door behind us.

Birdie grabbed my hand and gave it a squeeze. She had a very respectable grip. It sure got my attention. "Corette, this is Princess Jayne."

Corette curtseyed. "Your Highness."

"Oh, wow, no need for that." I almost rolled my eyes at Birdie and her princess business. "Please, just call me Jayne. I'm sorry about your shop. And thank you so much for the cover story about the signs being reversed. That was so nice of you."

"This is Nocturne Falls, my dear." Her smile was warm and welcoming. "Things happen. Granted, those things aren't always this drastic, but we learn to deal with such occurrences. And we watch out for each other." Corette clasped her hands in front of her. "Now, let's see what we can do about getting this magic back in its box, shall we? Come into my office."

Birdie and I followed her back and settled into the chairs in front of her desk. I took the box out and placed it in front of Corette.

She examined it as I told her what I'd recently found out. "It held a chaos imp and was intended for one of Francine Gresham's clients."

"Sentient magic," Corette answered. She shook her head. "Often considered a gray area for most witches. And sometimes, darker than that."

"Meaning?"

She pursed her lips. "Sentient magic is anything that can think for itself. Of course, thinking is a

149

broad term. Most imps don't process much thought beyond what havoc they can wreak and where to get the energy they need. They're part of the jinn family and within that family are various levels of creatures. Genies being the most advanced."

Like Imari. "Where do imps fall in those levels?"

"Closer to the bottom of that list. Which is beneficial in our case. As I said, they're not deep thinkers and, with some skill, should be relatively easy to catch. Well, perhaps easy isn't the right word, but it did end up in this box at some point, didn't it? Recapturing it won't be a walk in the park, but it's definitely doable."

"So what do you suggest?"

She frowned apologetically. "Nothing immediately. Because this is gray magic, it's not something I'm very familiar with. I'm sure you have gifts that could easily allow you to circumvent certain laws, but doing so would be wrong. Therefore, you don't. Which means you understand what's possible, but most likely not how to put such things into practice."

I tried to keep my expression neutral, but thoughts of my previous breaking-and-entering escapades popped into my head.

She continued. "For me, that means while I know about gray and black magic, I don't practice it, so I'm not well versed in the peculiarities of it. I'll have to do some research."

Birdie sighed. "I guess we'll have to come back."

Corette held up a finger. "Give me a moment." She moved the box toward the edge of the desk, then took out a key, unlocked a drawer in a cabinet behind her and, with some effort, removed a large book bound in scarred leather and adorned with unusual gold markings and metal corners. A title was scrolled across the front, but it seemed to be Latin and in that fancy script, so I couldn't read it upside down.

She placed the book carefully in the space she'd cleared and gave it a little pat. "One of my daughters returned this grimoire to me yesterday thinking it might contain something that would help me restore my dresses to their rightful color. Unfortunately, not all of the imp's spells can be undone as easily as lifting a fire truck off of a building."

"Oh, did you help with that? Thank you so much. Cooper was so upset by that. Cooper Sullivan, that is. He's a fireman. And an old friend. He's a summer elf." And I was rambling. I smiled. "Sorry. You were saying?"

Her mouth bent in an understanding way. "Is Cooper also your beau?"

"My—oh no. Well. Not exactly. It's complicated."

Her grin widened. "Love often is."

Love? Was she snowing me? I shook my head. "I wouldn't say it's love."

She just nodded. "When you're ready for a wedding dress, let me know. I would be honored to assist you with that. If your dress isn't already chosen, of course. I know things can be different with royalty."

"No, I don't have a dress yet. And I think it's going to be a while before I need one." A long while. Like years. Wow. Talk about changing the conversation. "If we could go back to the imp problem…"

"Of course." She opened the book and began turning pages. "If you'll just give me a moment."

I squinted at the book, then glanced at Birdie and frowned. Birdie frowned back and shrugged. I couldn't keep quiet. "Pardon me for saying anything, Corette, but those pages look blank to me. Is that some kind of spell doing that?"

Corette glanced up, amusement in her gaze. "Very good. Yes, it's a protection spell, meant to keep our secrets from the uninitiated."

"Nicely done." I nodded and sat back to wait. Protective magic was what kept the North Pole hidden from humans. And it kept my uncle safe on Christmas Eve. If anyone could appreciate protective magic, it was me.

After a few minutes of flipping through the book and making small sounds of consternation, she stopped at a page and tapped it. "This mentions imps briefly, but it's mostly about how to avoid accidentally summoning one since that spell is very similar to another spell used to entice ladybugs and fireflies into one's yard."

My brows lifted. "Is that done very often? Calling ladybugs and fireflies?"

Corette gave a little shrug. "For green witches, like my daughter Marigold, yes, I imagine it would be."

"Does it say anything else about imps?"

"Let me read a little further." She went quiet for a few moments as her finger underlined words I couldn't see. "Mostly it says that they're attracted to the sugar used in the insect spell. It seems sugar is their main source of energy."

It was kind of mine, too. "So…maybe I could put sugar in the box and the imp would come back?"

She loosened the ribbon attached to the book's spine and laid it over the page before closing the book. "I don't think it will be that easy, but it's worth a shot."

"I was afraid you'd say that." I picked up the box and put it back in the tote bag. "Any thoughts on how to do this? Should I really just put sugar in the box?"

Birdie piped up. "You'll probably need to leave the window open."

Corette nodded. "Could be. Was your window open when the lid got knocked off?"

I tried to remember. "No. But I opened it right after it happened. Spider, my cat, started talking because of the imp and when I first heard his voice, I pushed the window up to see if someone was fooling around on the fire escape."

"That's how the imp got out of your apartment, then," Corette said. "And you didn't see anything?"

"Nothing other than the green stuff left inside."

"So the imp can become invisible. Or perhaps that's its natural state." Corette peered into the distance, clearly thinking something over. Then she looked at me again. "I may not be able to counteract all of its magic, but I believe I can come up with a spell to make it permanently visible. I'll need a sample of the residue in the box, if that's all right with you."

I took the box out again and handed it over. "Absolutely."

She took the lid off, then used a bone letter opener from her pen cup to scrape a bit of the green stuff onto a sheet of paper. She folded the paper neatly and tucked it into her handbag. "That ought to do."

"You sure that's enough?"

"Yes." She put the lid back on and handed the box to me. "Tonight, leave your window open. Doesn't have to be much, a half inch should be plenty. I have a feeling an imp such as this could slip through a much smaller opening. Put a small dish of sugar in the box. A thimble would work."

"How about a bottle cap?"

"Perfect. Then, first thing in the morning, if the sugar's gone, even if you don't see anything in the box, close the lid carefully and quietly."

"Why do I have to wait until tonight?"

"You don't, but I think that's your best chance. Imps are mostly nocturnal. And according to the grimoire, the imp should sleep for a bit after feeding so when you put the lid on, be careful not to wake it. Just remember that even if you don't see it in the box, with its ability to be invisible, it could very well be in there."

"But if it's invisible, how will I know if I've caught it?"

She smiled. "Bring the box back to me. Or I'll come to you. Either way, I'll be able to tell. Any witch would. The presence of that much magic would be hard to ignore."

A thought popped into my head. "Do you think Francine's client could be a witch? Maybe one not powerful enough to summon an imp on her own but someone who has a need for that kind of magic?"

Corette tipped her head. "It's possible, but as I mentioned, imps are gray magic at best. We don't allow dabbling in such arts in our coven, so if the imp was for someone local, they certainly aren't going to talk about it. However, it's a possibility. I'll ask around and see what I can find out."

"That would be great. I'll give you my number." I fished out a business card from my purse and handed it over.

"And I'll give you mine." Corette took my card, then lifted one of the shop's from the holder on her desk and offered it in exchange. "Call me anytime, night or day."

I took the card. "Likewise. And thank you. That's very kind of you. And I appreciate your time. Which reminds me that I need to get back to work."

"I imagine we all do." She stood and extended her hand. "We're all in this together, Jayne. Don't forget that."

Birdie and I got to our feet, and I took Corette's hand. "I'm glad to hear that, because this imp stuff is so not my area."

"Well, Birdie was right to bring you here." She walked us to the door and unlocked it. "If all goes well, I'll be talking to you soon."

"I hope you're right. And again, I'm sorry about your dresses."

Her smile was patient and kind. "A new order came in last night. I'll make do with those until this is all sorted out. It's just life in Nocturne Falls."

We said good-bye, then Birdie walked as far with me as the police station, where she thanked me again for breakfast and made me promise to keep her updated, which I did.

From the sheriff's department, I went straight to my office. I was fifteen minutes late as it was. I hung the tote bag on the coat rack and tossed my purse in a drawer. I was about to head into the store to let Juniper and Kip know I was in when I noticed the snow globe on my desk had a full-on raging blizzard inside it.

I sat down at my desk, picked up the globe, and pushed the button to accept the call. My dad's face appeared. His dark blue brows were knit together in an unhappy expression.

"Hi, Dad."

"What's going on? Are you all right? I've been trying to reach you for hours. It's times like this the inability to use electronics in the North Pole really irks me. Has something happened?" Wisps of icy vapor curled up around him, further evidence of his mood. He wasn't always the most patient of people.

"I'm fine, Dad. I'm sorry I've been out of touch, but…" I hadn't wanted to tell him about the imp, but I sort of had to now. "There's been a little development." I spilled the whole miserable story, making sure to bring him up to date so that he knew progress was being made toward fixing things.

His expression shifted to one of concern. "Sorry to hear that, Jay, but it wasn't your fault, and it sounds like you've got a good group of people helping you out. Is there anything I can do?"

"I don't think so. If Corette can work up a spell to make the imp visible, that will help a lot."

He looked unconvinced. "Maybe I should come down there when she does. I could freeze the whole town, then we could send out a troop of elves to search for the imp. Once we find it, we can just chip it free from wherever it's frozen and contain it."

"I appreciate the offer, but I don't think the Ellinghams would be too keen on that kind of climate change in August. A deep freeze like that could really hurt the tourist industry."

He hmphed. "I suppose so. But if you change your mind, let me know."

"I will." But that was not going to happen. The last thing I wanted to do was give the Ellinghams another reason to dislike me. "So...what were you trying to reach me about?"

"Hmm? Oh, yes. I just wanted to let you know there's a new shipment of toys coming to you today, and in some very exciting news, your uncle and I have decided that your store would be the perfect place to debut a new thing we have in the works. Won't be for a couple months, but we're going to make a big splash."

"Really? That's pretty cool." Especially considering that they'd almost shut down the Nocturne Falls location after so many employees had gone missing. They'd changed their minds after that mystery had been solved and I'd insisted on taking this store over, but this felt like a major vote of confidence. "What's the new toy?"

He winked at me. "This is all still in the final stages of development, but we're working with Sanders to come up with something incredible."

I stared at him. "Wow. That is big." Tempus Sanders, aka the Sandman, worked with my uncle Kris on Christmas Eve to assure that children across the world stayed asleep so that he could leave their presents undetected. Yes, I'm talking about *the* Sandman. The guy in charge of sleep. The Dream Maker. The King of Slumber. The Night Manager. The—well, you get the idea. "What's the toy?"

My dad's eyes twinkled. "Here's the thing. It's not a toy. It's a book. And it's unlike any book ever written. When a parent reads the book to their child, it guarantees the child will fall asleep before the end and they'll sleep peacefully the whole night. It's revolutionary. And it will only be available at our stores. At least initially."

"Revolutionary is right. That's going to create a huge buzz." I could only imagine how many parents were going to want a book like that.

"I'm glad you think so, because we're sending Sanders to Nocturne Falls for the week of the launch. He'll do signings and readings in the store."

"Oh." I swallowed. That was more than I could instantly process. I mean, Sanders *here*? At my store? With me in charge? That was huge.

A little of the joy melted off my father's face. "We just thought if anything *unusual* happened, Nocturne Falls would be the perfect town to handle it. After all, they have that bespelled water that keeps humans from noticing odd things." He shrugged. "Seemed like a good idea."

"No, it's a great idea. You're absolutely right." So long as that bespelled water wasn't still Dr Pepper in a couple months. "The store will be crazy busy when word about that book gets out."

"We think so too, which is why we've already discussed sending you extra help for that week. In fact, we're probably going to pull a few top employees from other locations. That way you won't have to train anyone new and those employees will get the reward of being part of the launch. And he'll have his assistant with him most likely, so you're not going to have to cater to him. It's a win-win."

I nodded. It was also a lot of responsibility. The Sandman was kind of a rock star in the elf world. Not as big as my dad or my uncle, but a close second, definitely. And even with an assistant to help him, I had no doubt it was going to be an intense week. "It'll be great."

"I'll let you know more details as we get closer, honey."

"Thanks."

"I hope you catch the imp soon."

I sighed as his words brought me back to my immediate problem. "Me too."

We hung up. I put the globe back on the desk corner, then pulled out the container of snickerdoodle toffee cookies my mother had sent and powered down three of them. Okay, maybe it was five, but let's not get hung up on numbers. Buoyed by the sugar, I put the cookies away, my dad's news behind me, and headed into the shop.

Kip was at the register, and Juniper was fixing a display of Magic Eight Balls by the door.

"How's it going? Any fires to put out?" I really hoped the answer to that last question was no.

Kip shook his head. "Easy day so far. But then, we haven't been open that long."

"Right." I looked at Juniper.

She shrugged. "Nothing to report here either." Then her eyes narrowed. "You okay? You look...stressed."

"Can't imagine why." I laughed. A little hysterically. "No, I'm good. It's just this whole imp thing."

"Imp?" Juniper's eyes widened. "Is that what was in the box?"

"Yes. Crazy right?"

Kip made a face. "I'm not even sure what an imp is."

"I wasn't either until this happened. It's a kind of mischievous magical creature, sentient magic, I've been told. Anyway, it's what's causing all the weird stuff happening in town."

He nodded. "Like the fountain in the center of town? Or was that a store promotion?"

My stomach dropped. "What happened to the fountain?"

"It's spraying snow instead of water. I went down to the Hallowed Bean to get coffees for Juniper and me before work this morning and walked right past it. The gargoyle on duty didn't seem too happy about it, but the tourists were loving it. Especially the kids!"

Sure they were. Because who wouldn't like a little snow in the middle of summer in Georgia? At least this prank wasn't so bad. But just like with the falls turning into Dr Pepper, this trick definitely looked connected to me. I was surprised I hadn't had a call from Hugh Ellingham yet. "I'll be in my office if anyone needs me."

I started to leave, then stopped and turned around. "Forgot to mention, we're getting a shipment of toys today. I haven't looked to see if they're in yet so they could be. They'll need to be checked in and put on display."

"I'm all over it," Juniper said. "And I'll show Kip the process, because we haven't done that yet."

"Except you can't both be in the warehouse at the same time. That'll leave the store empty." I really needed that fifth employee. I should have reminded my dad about that. "Tell you what, I'll see if the toys are here. If they are, I'll watch the store and you guys can handle the new inventory."

"You sure, boss?" Kip asked. "I can always learn the system on the next batch."

"No, this'll be fine." Honestly, working in the shop would be a great distraction. "I'll be right back."

I retreated into the warehouse. Maybe it was odd, but I really liked the big, dim space with its racks of inventory. It was cool and quiet and strangely tranquil. I stood there for a moment, in between my office and the vestibule that led to the street door, and just took a few deep breaths. My plate wasn't just full, it was overflowing, but I was the Winter Princess. I could handle this.

Besides being the Winter Princess, I was also the manager of this shop. So really, it was my job to handle all of this. And if my parents and my aunt and uncle believed I was equipped to be in this position, then I was.

The little pep talk did me some good. I walked

the rest of the way to the Santa's Bag, but I could already tell it was empty. I returned to the shop and stuck my head in. "Nothing yet. I'll check again in a bit, but I'm taking a quick fifteen in case you need me."

Kip gave me the thumbs-up.

I went back to my office and did what I should have done when I first got in. I took the box upstairs to my apartment.

I pulled it out of the tote bag and yanked the lid off. I set both pieces on the table, then walked into the kitchen and took a Dr Pepper out of the magically replenished stock in the fridge. After a few long drinks, I left the bottle on the counter but took the cap to the box. It fit inside easily.

I filled it with sugar from the bowl on the table, careful not to spill any in the box. Then I cracked the window about an inch.

Spider had yet to come see me, so I walked back into the bedroom to find him. He was sprawled on the bed, a catnip mouse next to him. The little druggie.

I gave his belly a rub. "Spider, wake up. It's just me this time."

He blinked a few times, then yawned and finally looked at me. "Sleepy."

"Yes, I know I'm interrupting your very important eleventh nap of the day, but listen. I have the window in the living room open a bit and the box the imp came out of is on the table. Inside the box is a soda cap full of sugar. Don't spill it, don't knock it over, don't play with it. Don't touch it. Understand? It's supposed to draw the imp, and if it returns and I can catch it, then all the town's troubles will be solved."

He stuck his paws in the air and made biscuits in response to my continued belly rubs, which was cute, but really called into question whether or not he'd been paying attention. "Spider, did you hear what I was saying?"

"No touch sugar."

Close enough. "Very good. Go back to sleep now." I kissed his silky little head and went downstairs to my office. Still nothing in the Santa's Bag. Even so, I went into the store, grabbed a green apron and went to work. Mostly I cleaned shelves, dusted and straightened stock. It was a good way to lose myself for a few hours.

It also allowed Juniper and Kip to take lunch without any trouble. And I was happy to be in the store. I really enjoyed it. Seeing the kids' faces light up at the sight of all the toys was always a treat.

But that activity wasn't enough to make me forget the other oddness that had popped up today. The text from Lark. As I worked, I wondered if it was possible that the text was another of the imp's jokes. Had she really texted me? Because if I texted back out of the blue, that could start a conversation between us, and I really didn't feel ready for that.

What did you say to the woman you'd once considered your best—and maybe only—friend but had actually turned out to be the reason you and the love of your life broke up? I mean, she'd deliberately made Cooper and I believe lies about each other. And all with the intention of ending our relationship (job done) so that she could have Cooper for herself (job not done). If I went the rest of my life without talking to her, I'd be okay. Sad. But okay.

The only way I could know if Lark's text was the real deal was to talk to Cooper. Kip and Juniper were both back from lunch, so I said I was going to check the Santa's Bag again, then slipped into the warehouse.

The Santa's Bag was full, but the new inventory could sit for a few minutes longer. I took out my phone, tapped his name on my contacts list and listened to it ring.

"Hey, Jay. What's up? Don't tell me you're calling to cancel tonight."

"I'm not."

"Good, because we really need to talk."

"I might know why. Any chance you want to tell me now?"

He sighed. "I hate to even mention her name, but I got a text from Lark."

"Snowballs. So did I. That's why I called you. I

wasn't sure if it was real or another one of the imp's pranks."

"Hmm. I guess it's possible he pranked both of us with it."

"How do we know for sure?"

"I don't have a clue. But let's figure it out over dinner this evening. I'm supposed to be helping the guys wash the truck."

"And I have new stock to check in. Dinner it is. Howler's at seven?"

"Sounds good. See you then, beautiful."

I smiled. "Bye, handsome."

I hung up, no more sure who the text had come from. How would the imp know about Lark? I went back into the shop. "Kip, the new shipment is here. You want to grab Juniper and have her show you how we check it in and shelve it?"

"You got it."

As he went to get Juniper from the back of the store, I took his spot behind the register and let my thoughts take over. This Lark thing had me stumped. If the text was real, what on earth could she want?

The question stuck in my head all day. I worked almost until six, trying to catch up with my paperwork and get ahead in anticipation of how distracted I was going to be until this imp was caught. But the Lark question was always there, pestering me like a loose tooth. Or a burnt tongue.

It was a nuisance I couldn't get rid of. Even as I headed up to my apartment to get ready for dinner, it remained answerless.

But standing at my door reminded me that I had something else to consider. The imp. And whether or not my trap had worked.

Opening the door could startle the little creature. Maybe scare it right back out the window. I had to be sly and quiet, and there was only one way to get into my place without making any noise.

I had to use my inherited skill of stealth entering. Or as I liked to call it, the Saint Nick Slide. The magical ability was something I'd gotten from my mom's side of the family. It worked like this: so long as there was a break in the structure, like where a door closed or a window met the sill, or yes, a chimney, I could enter pretty much any space.

That ability was about to become super handy. All it took was a shimmer of magic and a couple seconds of feeling oddly compressed, followed by an uncomfortable nausea, and there I was, on the inside of my apartment.

I took a moment to breathe through the urge to hurl. How Uncle Kris did that all night long on Christmas Eve I had no earthy clue. It made me feel like I was on the downward part of a really steep roller coaster.

The dizziness cleared, so I tiptoed to the kitchen

table and peeked into the box. The sugar didn't look like it had been touched. I frowned, disappointed, even though Corette had said imps were nocturnal.

Getting out of the house for a few hours for dinner could be a good thing. With that thought as my focus, I changed into jeans and a T-shirt and my now-standard flip-flops. Cute but definitely not the kind of cute I put on for Greyson. Hmm.

I added a little extra eye makeup, a slick of bright gloss and ran a brush through my hair. But then my face didn't match my outfit. I headed back to my closet and found a floral peasant blouse that was just as comfortable as a tee but a lot prettier. And pulled down off my shoulders, it was borderline sexy.

The jeans and flip-flops stayed, but the look worked. I topped off Spider's kibble, checked on the sugar in the box again (nothing new), then grabbed my purse and made my way to Howler's. It was moderately busy, but not so crowded there weren't seats at the bar. I slid into one since I was early, which was saying something considering I was meeting Cooper.

Bridget, the owner and bartender (and werewolf), greeted me with a nod. She leaned on the bar in front of me and tossed a towel over her shoulder. We'd gotten to know each other by name since the first time I'd come in here and she'd directed me to the supernaturals-only nightclub where I'd met Greyson. "I heard you and my aunt had breakfast this morning."

Further proof that everyone knew everything in a small town. "We did. I really like Birdie. She's…I don't know. Pretty awesome." I laughed. "You're very lucky to have her as an aunt."

Bridget smiled. "I think so too. She loves you, by the way." Bridget's eyes narrowed. "Is it true that your father is Jack Frost, the Winter King? And you're a princess?"

"Yep. Guilty as charged."

Bridget looked impressed. "Wow, that's wild." She shrugged. "Birdie sometimes exaggerates."

"Not this time. But I don't get too hung up on the title. The one that means more to me right now is manager of Santa's Workshop."

Bridget took the towel off her shoulder and wiped down the bar in front of me. "I totally get it. My father is the alpha of the Georgia Pack. Not that that's anything like being the Winter King—"

"I don't know. Sounds pretty impressive."

"I guess, but you know how it is. When you grow up with that, it's just status quo."

"Uh huh. I know what you mean."

"Anyway, nice to have you in town. What can I get you? You want a menu?"

"Just a drink. I'm meeting someone for dinner, but I'm early."

"Sure thing. What's your poison?"

"White wine. That moscato one."

She grinned. "You like the sweet stuff, huh?"

"It's a winter elf thing."

"You got it." She headed off to get my drink, coming back with a glass that was generously full.

"Thank you."

"You're welcome." She looked past me toward the entrance and gave a little wave, her face erupting in a huge smile. "Hey, bro. Hi, Sam."

I twisted my barstool halfway around to look. Cooper had just walked in with two other men in fireman's uniforms. The one guy I recognized as his boss, the other one must have just been Sam.

Cooper winked at me and started in my direction. I wiggled my fingers at him as I glanced at Bridget. "That's right, your brothers are the sheriff and the fire chief, right?"

Pride lit her face. "Yep. Hank and Titus Merrow are my brothers. And Sam is my guy. He's also Hank's wife's brother. It's a little weird, but we're making it work. Hey, is Cooper your date?"

I didn't want to go into the whole thing about it not being a date, because it sort of was, so I just nodded.

She grinned. "Coop's a catch. And for a non-shifter, super hot."

"He's a summer elf. Hot is his middle name."

"Talking about me again?" Cooper put a hand

on the back of my barstool and gave me a smolder that would have instantly dissolved most women's undies. I glanced down to make sure nothing was smoking. It wasn't. Yet.

"Are you going to introduce me?" I tipped my head toward the chief and Sam standing next to him.

Cooper's expression said he knew I was changing the subject on purpose. "Chief and Sam, this is Jayne Frost. Chief, you met at the fundraiser a couple months ago, but she lives here now. Jayne, this is my boss, Chief Titus Merrow."

"Hey," Sam said. Then he leaned in to kiss Bridget.

Chief Merrow nodded at me. "Nice to see you again, Miss Frost. Or should I say Princess?"

I groaned. "Let me guess. You talked to your aunt today."

He smiled wryly. "I did. You made quite an impression."

"Well, so did she."

His smile faded. "I was happy to hear the current *situation* may be rectified soon."

Stupid imp. "As soon as it possibly can be. I'm sorry about your fire truck. I'm glad you were able to get it down without too much trouble."

He nodded. "Me, too. Now if we can get everything else back to normal…"

I held my hands up. "I'm working on it, I swear."

"Titus, cut her some slack," Bridget said. "She didn't do it on purpose."

A soft light came into the chief's eyes as he looked at his sister. "I know. Really, if anyone's to blame, it's Francine Gresham."

He glanced at me again. "I didn't mean to imply the fault was yours. Frankly, I'm happy Francine is moving out of town. She and Roger always seemed to be at odds with what Nocturne Falls was about." He shook his head. "Enough on that subject. I'll let you and Cooper get on with your date. Nice to meet you again, Jayne."

"You too, Chief. And Sam." Once again, I let the date comment slide. "Cooper, I just need to pay for my wine and we can get a table."

"It's on the house," Bridget said. She shrugged one shoulder. "It's not every day I meet a princess."

Cooper and I settled into the last available booth. I sipped my wine while he ordered a beer.

When the server left to get his drink, I opened my menu, but my eyes were on him. "How was your day?"

"Okay." He looked a little tired, which did nothing to distract from his epic hotness and kind of made me want to offer my lap as a place to lay his head. "The crazy calls keep coming in."

I was almost afraid to ask. "Like what?"

"Today, the gym at the elementary school was filled with frogs, a hydrant on Broom was oozing lime Jell-O, and the fountain in the center of Main Street park spewed snow all over the place."

I cringed. Frogs weren't my favorite creatures. "I heard about the fountain. We had several customers ask if it was a promotion for the store."

"I wondered about that myself, but there was

175

no permit on file, so I knew it had to be the imp."

"I really am trying to get that thing back under control."

"I know." Then he shrugged. "Keeps the day interesting, I'll say that much. How was your day? Miss me?"

"Maybe." Then I batted my lashes at him. "Actually, I was too busy to miss anyone today. Being manager is a lot of work."

"And I bet you're amazing at it. How are your folks? They coming to visit any time soon?"

Was he angling to meet my parents or just making small talk? I had no idea. But it reminded me of our college days and how almost meeting my parents then had played into us breaking up. "No definite plans, but I'm sure they'll make their way here soon enough."

The server returned with Coop's beer, then pulled a notepad from her apron. "Y'all ready to order?"

"Not yet," Cooper said.

"I'll give you a few more minutes, then." She put the notepad away and went on to her next table.

He lifted his beer. "Here's to dinner with my favorite winter elf."

I smiled at that and clinked my glass against his. "Thanks. It's nice to see you too."

We both drank, then I stared at the menu. The

words didn't really register, mostly because of the elephant in the room. I decided to stop ignoring it. "What are we going to do about Lark?"

He sighed and looked up. "That question's been stuck in my head most of the day."

"Mine too."

He put his menu down. "How do you feel about her? Are you mad?"

"Of course I'm mad." Did he think I wasn't? "She broke us up, Coop. If not for her, who knows where we'd be right now."

A brightness filled his gaze. A look that seemed very much like hope to me. He nodded. "But we both agree we're different people now. We might have broken up anyway."

"True. But then it would have been on our terms. And based on reality, not lies." I stabbed my finger against the tabletop. "And let's not gloss over the fact that she tried to seduce you."

His lip curled as though the memory was replaying in his head. "Found her in my dorm room bed. No way to misunderstand that." He drank his beer, then tipped the mouth of the bottle at me. "But you two were friends. Best friends. You have a bigger dog in this hunt."

"Which is exactly what makes her behavior so awful. I can't forgive her for that kind of betrayal. Can you?"

His expression went very hard. "She took you

away from me, Jay. You know how I feel about that. How I felt about you then. How I feel…now."

I reached across the table and took his hand. I didn't know quite what to say to him in that moment, but the emotion in his words needed some kind of response. The years might have changed us, but we had shared history that would forever connect us.

He laced his fingers with mine. "I can't forgive her either. And you may not want to hear this, but if that text really is from her, I don't think reconnecting with her can be a good thing for either of us."

"What if she just wants to say she's sorry?"

"Great, but why wait so long? College was almost ten years ago. All of a sudden she wants to make amends?"

I took my hand back as I shifted in my seat. "Maybe she's dying. Maybe it's one of those things where she wants to apologize so she can end things with a clean slate. Or maybe she became an addict and is on one of the twelve steps of her recovery. Or she somehow found out that we know what she did and is trying to get proactive."

He snorted. "Your mind goes to some morbid places, but you might be on to something." He paused. "Does that mean you're willing to hear her out?"

I sighed. "I really don't know."

He ran his nail under the edge of the beer bottle's label. "You want me to handle it? I will. I can suss out what she wants, and then you can decide based on what I find out. For all she knows, you're still in the NP and unable to get the text anyway. Even summer elves know the Pole has notoriously spotty cell service."

"True." I thought about that. "Maybe that's the best thing." I glanced at my menu with genuine intent this time. But that didn't last long. "Actually, that won't work. Her text to me said she knew I was in the States. And that she hoped everything was chill. No clue what *that's* supposed to mean. What did yours say?"

He took out his phone and scrolled through his messages. "It says, *'This is a drive by texting from Lark. Remember me, Coop?'* Then a smiley face emoji."

"That's it?"

He put his phone down. "Yep. Sounds like a pretty open invitation to chat to me."

I squinted at him. "Really? Because to me it sounds light and flirty and like the only invitation she wants is into your pants."

He laughed out loud. "Do my eyes deceive me or do you look a little green?"

"Please. I'm not the jealous type." But I so could be. I tried to drink my wine nonchalantly. Which was harder to do than you'd think.

His smirk stayed firmly in place, but the twinkle in his eyes was new. "So you wouldn't care if I invited other women to my pants party?"

"Oh, it's a party now?"

He shrugged like he was bearing up under a great burden. "I don't know if you understand the effect this uniform has on women. It's a rare day that I don't come home with at least one phone number."

I could feel little ice crystals crunching through my veins. But I also knew Cooper was doing this on purpose. He enjoyed teasing me. Always had. "Is that so? And how many of them do you call?"

He stared at me, his gaze hot and deep. "Not a single one. Not since you came to town."

The ice crystals melted and I was left speechless again.

Fortunately, the server returned to take our order. I was so flustered, I started to ask for a salad. Salad! "Wait, no. Ignore that. I'll have that bacon mac-and-cheese casserole."

Cooper grinned but kept his eyes on the menu. "I'll have a cheeseburger and fries."

The server took our menus and left.

We sat there in silence for so long I finally had to say something. "You could, you know. If you wanted to."

"Could what?"

"Call one of those numbers."

One of his brows lifted. "You really mean that?"

I used the tines of my fork to draw lines on my paper napkin. "You know I'm seeing Greyson. There's no reason for you not to see whoever else you want. It would only be fair."

"Does the vampire date other women too, then?"

"I...don't know." We hadn't really discussed it. After all, the thing with Greyson and I was very new. We had none of the history that Cooper and I did.

Cooper leaned in. "Then let me make one thing very clear. Seeing other women might be all right for him, but it's not for me. You merit my full attention, Jay. A second chance with you is not something I'm going to half-ass. No matter where you're at with us, that's where I'm at. And you deserve to know that. You need to know that. Because at some point, it's going to matter."

That was sweet and flattering and a little scary. I did my best not to react too much. "That doesn't feel fair to you, though. Not when I'm not ready to commit."

"Babe, one of these days you're going to wake up and know which one of us you want. It's inevitable, and I'm content to wait. So long as that wait includes time with you. Hell, I could do this for the next fifty years if I had to." He took a slow pull off his beer, then put it down and smiled. "I'm a very patient man."

He was also extremely easy to be with. Our food

arrived, and he shifted the conversation away from all the relationship talk to tell me stories about his time as a fireman. He kept me laughing and entertained all the way through dinner and the walk home.

At my door, he lifted my chin and stared into my eyes. "Thank you for meeting me tonight. I know you're busy and bogged down with this imp issue, so don't worry about Lark. I'll deal with it and let you know what happens, okay?"

"Okay." I was a little high on his charm and sweetness at the moment. As much as I needed to go upstairs and go to bed, I wasn't ready for things to end just yet. "You can kiss me now."

"As you wish, Princess." He smiled a little lopsided smile, then put his mouth on mine and did just that. The kiss was long and slow and hot but filled with the kind of restraint that drove me crazy. How he had such control when I felt like I was coming apart at the seams, I had no idea. But then he'd always been the master of the tease, able to make me crazy with a single touch or a heated glance or a kiss that verged on reckless but didn't quite fall completely off the edge. It was school days all over again. We could have been standing outside my dorm.

But we weren't kids anymore. And if I didn't break this kiss off soon, we were going to end up doing some very adult things.

I stepped back, trying to catch my breath. "I should go to bed."

His smile was back, this time wickedly bent. "I'm going to assume that's not another invitation and say good night."

I nodded, still stupefied by the brand his mouth had left on mine. "Uh huh. Bed. I mean, night."

He tipped his head toward the door. "I'll wait until you're in."

I wandered over to the door, pulled my key out and unlocked it. "Thanks again for dinner."

"My pleasure."

I sucked in a breath and went inside, smiling and warm. Whatever stress I'd been feeling before dinner was completely gone. I floated up to my apartment and completely forgot about entering quietly until I shut the door behind me.

"Snowballs." If the imp had been here, I'd probably scared him off. I checked the sugar. It was all there and still looked untouched. Maybe it wasn't going to work. That was a depressing thought.

I refused to let that bring me down. It would work. I'd wake up in the morning and the little invisible wretch would be passed out in the box. Cooper had left me far too happy to think otherwise.

With the taste of his kiss still fresh on my lips, I got ready for bed, gathered Spider up and went to sleep.

But morning brought no miraculous good news. There wasn't a crystal of sugar out of place in that soda cap. I frowned and pushed hair out of my face. "This isn't working."

Then I wrinkled my nose. Something in the apartment was super stinky. Like cat food gone bad. But there wasn't a morsel in Spider's wet-food bowl.

I sniffed the trash. Nothing there either. Finally, I shoved the window all the way up to let some fresh air in. And nearly gagged.

I had a pretty good idea what new trouble the imp had caused. I shut the window again. Great. I was definitely going to hear about this one. Having the whole town smell like week-old tuna was *not* going to be good for business.

Spider rubbed up against my leg. "Hungry. Mama feed Spider."

"Yeah, yeah, I know the drill. Do you ever think about anything besides food?"

"Chicken Party."

"That is food, silly." I got his breakfast, then leaned on the counter drinking a Dr Pepper and trying to think about anything but the town reeking like a bait shop.

About halfway through the bottle, an idea came to me. Call Corette. So I did. Actually, I sent her a text. *Sugar hasn't been touched. Any new info? Besides the way the town smells.*

I left my phone on the counter and went to shower. By the time I was out, she'd responded.

The smell is awful, isn't it? But the covens will have it solved shortly. Try another type of sweet maybe. Still working on the visibility spell. Hope to finish it today.

Thank you! I texted back. *For both things!*

Having the coven take care of the smell made me feel instantly better, and with Cooper handling whatever was going on with Lark, and Corette helping me with the imp, my mind focused on the still unanswered question of who was Francine's client and why had they wanted that imp?

That felt like super important info to me. This imp was trouble. I couldn't imagine anyone using it for something good. But I could definitely imagine someone using it for all kinds of bad reasons. And revenge felt like it was at the top of that list.

If that was the case, wouldn't the imp-buyer still be looking to get that revenge? Someone in Nocturne Falls could be facing danger from something other than a chaos imp.

Feeling a new sense of urgency while I got ready for the day, I mulled how to get my hands on Francine's client list. If I could talk to whoever was on the list in Nocturne Falls, I might get a sense for who'd been out for revenge, although it was possible her imp-obsessed client didn't live here.

Problem was, Francine would never willingly give me that list. And trying to get it by some legal means might result in her destroying it. Or creating a fake one.

And she was moving. Based on how packed-up her house was, she might already be gone.

There was only one way I could think of to get my hands on that list.

I frowned at myself in the mirror. Looked like my breaking-and-entering days weren't over yet.

I called Birdie. She answered right away.

"Good morning, Princess! How are you this fine day?"

"I'm, uh, I'm fine. Birdie, Jayne, please. And I have a question for you."

"Oh yes, yes. Jayne. Of course. Ask away, I'm happy to help."

"Do you have any idea how much longer Francine is going to be in town?"

"No, but I think I know how to find out. I'll need to get into the office first and check on a few things. I'll call you back as soon as I have an answer."

"Perfect. Thank you." No clue how she was going to find out, but Birdie seemed to have access to intel that others didn't. Of course, she *did* work in the sheriff's department. "I'll talk to you soon."

"Yes, you will. Have a good day, Princ—uh, Jayne."

"You too, Birdie." I hung up and got myself some breakfast, then I brushed my teeth, checked the sugar in the box one more time (no change) and headed down to the office.

I was seven minutes early, which was pretty good. It made me feel like I was really on top of things, but then I spent the next twenty minutes staring into space while I tried to figure out the best plan of action for getting into Francine's place without being caught. The woman was known for never leaving.

So I either had to do it at night, and hope she was sleeping, or I had to create a diversion that would get her out of the house.

If only the imp took direction.

I was still mulling that over when someone knocked on my office door. "Come in."

Juniper stuck her head in. "Hey, you busy?"

"Nope. And you don't need to knock. Just come in."

"Well, it's not just me. You have a visitor."

"Oh." I straightened a little. "Who is it?"

"Delaney Ellingham." Juniper grinned. "And she brought us a goodie box."

The box of goodies went into the employee break room (after Juniper and Kip helped themselves to a few select items), and Delaney and I settled into my office. Since I'd taken the space over and reorganized, I'd made room for a small love seat across from my desk, but this was the first time anyone who wasn't an employee had used it.

She took a seat there and I returned to my desk chair. "Can I get you something? Water? Coffee? Something else?" I almost cringed. Why had I said that? What if she asked for blood? She had to know I couldn't deliver on that request. Right?

"No, thank you, I'm fine."

I breathed a small sigh of relief. "Thank you again for the treats. That was really nice of you."

She smiled. "I know you're under a lot of pressure with this imp business. And you're already a good customer. I thought it would be a nice gesture. Plus, I wanted an excuse to drop by."

"You don't need an excuse. You're welcome any time. Your craftiness with sugar and chocolate gives you celebrity status in my eyes, so feel free."

She laughed. "Well, I'm glad you feel that way. I just wanted to check in and see how things were going. I heard through Stanhill that you'd been to see Corette and that she was working on a spell to make the imp visible. And that she'd given you a way to capture it."

I nodded. "Potentially. So far it hasn't worked. But it's only been one night."

"You're using sugar?"

"Yep. But tonight I'm going to try something different. Maybe pancake syrup. I'm not sure yet."

"Let me know if you want some samples of other sweeteners. I've got all kinds of stuff at the shop. Agave nectar, piloncillo, which is Mexican brown sugar. Let's see, what else…" She ticked the types off on her fingers. "Molasses, maple syrup, coconut sugar, corn syrup, although that one is sort of low on my list because it somehow feels so commercial to use that and I pride myself on things having a handcrafted touch."

"Speaking of homemade…" I took the container of my aunt's fudge out of my desk drawer and pried off the lid. "You should try this. It's eggnog fudge. I don't want to brag or anything, but getting a chance to taste this particular confection outside of the North Pole is a pretty rare treat."

Her eyes lit up. "Oh, I'd love to."

I held the box out. "I figure if anyone can appreciate its uniqueness, it's you."

She delicately lifted a piece with two fingers, then took a bite that cut the chunk cleanly in two. The next sound that came out of her was a soft moan. "Oh. Wow." Her eyes closed, and more happy noises spilled out of her. She swallowed and opened her eyes to look at the fudge. "This is insane. Is your aunt some kind of sugar goddess? This has to be magic."

I lifted one shoulder. "I wouldn't say she's a sugar goddess, but she *is* Santa Claus's wife, so—"

"Jumping jam cakes." Delaney's eyes widened. "Are you telling me I just ate fudge made by Mrs. Claus? Like, *the* Mrs. Claus?"

"Yep, that's my aunt."

"Wow. Just wow." She gestured at me with the hand holding the last half of the fudge. "This is absolutely the best fudge of any flavor I've ever had. No contest."

"That's high praise coming from you."

She popped the rest of the candy into her mouth and spent a few happy moments savoring it. When she was ready to speak again, she held up two fingers. "Two things. One, you should put a tiny piece of this into the box. If that doesn't draw the imp, we might be in worse trouble than we realize."

"Hey, that's a great idea. And one I totally should have thought of." But I'd been focused on straight-up sugar.

She waved that away. "You would have." Then her fingers came up again. "And two, I need this recipe. I have to have this in my shop for Christmas. Please ask your aunt. I'll happily bill it as Mrs. Claus's fudge and pay her whatever she wants for the recipe, or do some kind of split on the sales or whatever. But I need it."

"I don't know. My aunt won't even give my mother the recipe. It's a pretty closely guarded secret."

Delaney put her hand on her rounded belly and made puppy-dog eyes at me. "Think of how happy it would make the baby."

I snorted. "Is that even fair?"

She laughed. "The best part about being pregnant is you end up with a baby. The second best part of being pregnant is the perks that come with it." She hoisted herself off the love seat. "The last time I wanted something this badly, I ended up marrying him. Please talk your aunt into sharing this recipe with me."

I held my hands up as I stood. "I'll talk to her about it, but don't hold your breath. She's a tough cookie. No pun intended."

Delaney smiled. "Make sure you tell her I'm pregnant."

I shook my head and grinned. "You really do play dirty."

Her mouth pursed in a coy expression. "I just think she should have all the facts."

I chuckled as I opened the office door. "I'll make sure she knows."

"And I'll make sure to send over a sampling of all the sweet additives I can think of." She gave me a little wave as she left. "Something will draw that imp in sooner or later."

"Hopefully sooner. Thanks for stopping by." I shut the door and went back to my desk.

My phone rang as I sat down. "Santa's Workshop, Jayne speaking. How can I help you?"

"Princess Jayne, it's Birdie."

She'd managed to get my name in there, so I let the princess bit go. "Hi, Birdie. Did you find anything out?"

"Yes, but I'm not sure it's good news. Or maybe it is. I have no idea what answer you want."

"Maybe you could just tell me what you found out?"

"Oh, of course! According to the permits on file—see, for an eighteen-wheeler to enter that particular neighborhood, a permit has to be issued and the dates of arrival and departure have to be approved and registered with the sheriff's department. People in that neighborhood are very particular about these kinds of things. Actually, people in that neighborhood tend to be particular about a lot of things. Not all of them, mind you, but Francine definitely. It's understandable, I suppose. Well, for example, just the rumbling of the engine of a truck like that can rattle the glass in those old Victorian homes. I'm sure you can imagine—"

"Birdie?" I took a breath and reminded myself that this woman was helping me and very sweet and had no idea she was torturing me.

"Hmm?"

"Did you find out how much longer Francine is going to be in town? Or when she's moving?"

"Oh, yes! I'm so sorry, I do tend to ramble sometimes." I heard the clack of a keyboard. "According to the permits I pulled, there's a semi rolling into town two days from now. It's from Elite Movers and they're headed to her house. No doubt to load all her belongings and haul them off to wherever she's headed."

Two days was not a lot of time. "You think she'll be here at least until then, right?"

"Definitely. No way is a woman like Francine going to let her fancy-pants antiques and high-end household paraphernalia get loaded onto a truck without being there to supervise. But then she'll probably leave right after the truck does. No point in sticking around after that."

"Okay. Good enough."

Birdie cleared her throat, then lowered her voice. "Can I ask why you need this info?"

"You can ask...but I'm not sure I should tell you." I bit my lip. It wasn't that I didn't trust Birdie, but again, she worked at the sheriff's department. And I was technically about to commit a crime. A relatively harmless one, but still.

"What are you up to, Princess?"

I sighed. "I appreciate the info, but I don't want to involve you any further than I already have."

"Ahem." I could practically hear Birdie's drawn-on eyebrows lift. "Involve me any further in what?"

"Birdie, I just think this is a conversation better left unhad. Especially over the phone."

A long pause followed. "Are you at the shop?"

"Yes, but—"

"I'll be right over."

I shot forward. Like that was going to help. "Birdie, wait—"

The line went dead.

I hung up. This was getting far more complicated than I'd anticipated. My brain was starting to ache. I planted my elbows on my desk, then leaned my head into my hands. If Birdie figured out that I was going to break into Francine's and rifle through her stuff to see who wanted that imp, there was no way I could go through with it. I couldn't risk it.

My father might be willing to overlook a lot of things, but getting arrested was probably not one of them.

I sighed, then got up and walked over to the employee break room. The box from Delaney's shop beckoned. I opened it and stared into the chocolate abyss. It was glorious. I took a deep breath, the majestic aroma instantly relieving some of my stress.

I popped a truffle into my mouth, then snagged a small plate from the kitchenette and added a few more things, including a chocolate cupcake with what I hoped was peanut butter icing, and two frosted sugar cookies that were decorated to look like beach balls. The truffle dissolved on my tongue in a blissful mélange of dark chocolate and raspberry, sending my endorphins to a new, happier level.

The deliciousness also reinforced my belief that Delaney was a freaking genius with sweets. If there was anyone Aunt Martha was going to share her fudge recipe with, it should be her. At least it would be in safe hands. And Delaney could do it justice.

I went back to my office, plate in hand, and wrote myself a note to talk to my dad about getting Aunt Martha on the globe sometime this week.

Halfway through my daily batch of paperwork and all the way through my plate of snacks, Birdie opened my office door. "Am I interrupting?"

Even if I'd said yes, I wasn't sure it would have mattered. "No, come in."

She put a takeout bag with a large Styrofoam container in it on my desk. "I brought you some chili cheese fries from Mummy's."

I squinted at her, my mouth already watering. I could smell the fried, cheesy goodness. "Is this some kind of bribe?"

She sat in the same spot Delaney had just occupied. "Think of it more like edible persuasion."

I shook my head in disapproval. But took the box out and opened it anyway. What? You didn't turn down chili cheese fries from Mummy's. Not if you had an ounce of decency. I picked up one fry dripping with bright orange cheese sauce flecked with spicy bits of chili and popped it in my mouth. "I still can't tell you anything."

She frowned at me. "Why? Don't you trust me?"

"You work at the sheriff's department. And you're the sheriff's aunt."

She thought on that a moment. "So you're planning something illegal."

"Not exactly."

"And it involves Francine."

I groaned. I was having a hard time lying about this. "Birdie, please."

She shrugged. "I was going to see if you needed some help, but if you're going to take that kind of attitude, well, then, I guess we're not the friends I thought we were." Then she sniffed like she was on the verge of a cry.

Big hairy snowballs. "Birdie, you have to understand why someone wouldn't want to include you in their plans to hypothetically do something that might fall into a sort of legal gray area. Right?"

She crossed her arms. "I'm not the law. Hank is. And what he doesn't know won't hurt him." She uncrossed her arms and leaned closer. "In fact, having me involved might keep him from finding out."

I was on the horns of a dilemma here. I ate a few more fries while I thought it over. They were stupidly delicious. Or they were so delicious they were making me stupid. One of those. Finally, I held up my hands in surrender. "Okay. But is there any kind of confidentiality agreement we could come to?"

She pinched her fingers and ran them over her closed, smiling mouth. "My lips are sealed. Consider me at your service, Your Highness."

I bit the inside of my cheek, hoping the pain would keep me from laughing out loud. Her earnestness was endearing. "I was thinking I really need to have a look at Francine's files to see who she was buying that imp for. I mean, someone in town might be in danger. And if I could prevent that and didn't, and then something bad happened, well, I'd feel awful about it for the rest of my life."

Birdie gasped. "You're so right. We have to do this."

We? "Confiding in you doesn't mean you can tag along. I'm talking about breaking and entering."

"For a good cause! You'll be saving someone's life."

"That might be a bit of an exaggeration."

"You don't know that."

"True, but—"

"How are you going to get in? I think Hank has a lock-picking kit in his office somewhere. I can look for it."

"No, I already have a way in. If you're going to help at all, what I need is a lookout."

Her eyes lit up with an odd glow that I suddenly realized was her wolf shining out. "Oh, I can do that." She lifted her finger for emphasis. "We should have a signal. An alarm sound, in case someone shows up."

"Sure, that might—"

She tipped her head back and howled. Like, genuinely *howled*. I held on to the edges of my desk, slightly unnerved by the way the low, keening sound cut through me.

She finished and looked at me. "What do you think? That's the warning howl we use in the pack."

"Um…yeah, that would do it." Who was I to argue with a werewolf? "I don't think I'd be able to repeat it if I had to warn you about anything, though."

"Oh, you won't have to. You'll be inside the house. Nothing in there to worry about."

"Except Francine. Which leads me to the other sticking point in this whole scheme. Getting into her house with her still in it is going to be extra tricky. And I can't think of a way to make her leave."

That little shimmer of light reappeared in Birdie's gaze. "How long do you need inside the house?"

"Long enough to find the boxes holding her business stuff, then some more time to go through them and find the order lists. Half an hour minimum, I'd say."

"I can get you an hour. Maybe a little more."

Now that was impressive. "How?"

She lifted her chin a little. "Maybe I shouldn't tell you."

"Birdie."

She grinned. "I was thinking I could set up a fake meeting with her in Clarksville. That's about half an hour away. That would give you plenty of time."

"What kind of a fake meeting is going to get her to drive half an hour to meet someone she's never met?"

"Honey, I'm a werewolf. I have things that she'd like to buy."

I shook my head. "Such as?"

"My baby teeth, for one thing. Do you know what werewolf fangs go for on the black market?"

"Not a clue."

"Trust me. If I text her a picture of those, she'll meet me anywhere I ask her to. Once she gets to Clarksville, I'll let her stew for a few minutes, then text her that something else has come up and I have to cancel. Problem solved."

"Except what if she doesn't deal in relics? Greyson told me about them. They're definitely black market stuff."

"Oh, she'll bite. No pun intended."

"The other problem is she knows you live here in town. Why would she be willing to go all the way to Clarksville to meet you?"

"Because I'm not going to be me. I'm going to be someone else." She tipped her head. "I'll be Myrtis Lobb."

"The Peach Cobbler Queen?"

Birdie nodded slyly. "That name is as good as any other. And I'll use one of the burner phones Hank keeps around the station for undercover work, so she won't recognize the number." Birdie rolled her eyes. "Like we ever have undercover missions in Nocturne Falls."

I studied the woman across from me. "You're a lot more devious than I gave you credit for."

Her smile was wide and bright. "Never let it be said that Birdie Caruthers isn't a deep well of untapped talent."

"I'll say. Can you get this set up for tonight?"

She stood and settled the handle of her straw and bamboo handbag into the crook of her elbow. "You betcha. I'll text you when it's done. And then I'll see you tonight. We'll meet at the warehouse door at nine. If that works for you."

"It does. I'll see you then."

And just like that, I had a partner in crime.

Later that day, Corette called to say the visibility spell was in place and that she'd designed it so the imp would only be visible to supernatural eyes. She'd said word had been spread to keep a lookout, and if the imp was spotted, she'd let me know where. Then I told her about baiting the box with my aunt's fudge, and she agreed that was a great idea.

Other than that, the rest of my day was strictly store business. And a busier day in my office than I was used to. By the time I got back to my apartment, I was a little worn out. Fortunately, I had time for a quick nap before dinner and my *outing* with Birdie. First, I put some fudge in the still-untouched box, then I set my alarm for half an hour and lay down with Spider curled happily beside me.

When my alarm went off, I grabbed my phone

and sat up as I turned the beeping off. There were messages from Birdie, Greyson, and Cooper awaiting my attention. I scratched Spider's head while I scrolled through them. Birdie's was just confirming everything was a go and we were set for tonight. I had serious respect for what she'd pulled off. Getting Francine out of the house was going to make things so much easier.

Greyson wanted to know what I was up to, and Cooper's note was letting me know Lark had responded but we could talk about it tomorrow.

That made me curious. So naturally, I called him first. I got his voice mail. "Hey, Coop. I'm really curious to hear what you found out about Lark. Maybe we could get together sometime after work tomorrow. Let me know. Bye."

I hung up and texted Greyson. *I have plans with a friend. What are you up to?*

Then I texted Birdie a smiley face and a ninja emoji. That was the closest thing I could find to a burglar without actually texting something that might incriminate me.

Greyson answered. *What friend? The lifeguard?*

He's a fireman. And no. A female friend.

Winky face. *Have fun. I miss you already. Any chance for a night cap?*

I grinned. *Maybe.* After what I was about to get up to, I might really need a drink. *I'll text you when I'm home.*

Perfect. He signed off with a heart.

I tried not to read too much into that, but decided that if I did see him tonight, I would broach the subject of seeing other people so I could gauge his reaction. After Cooper's declaration that I was the only one for him regardless of how I felt in return, I confess I'd become pretty curious about where Greyson stood on the matter.

He was as extraordinarily handsome as Cooper was, just in a very opposite way. Greyson was dark, mysterious and a little dangerous, whereas Cooper was light, open and made me feel protected. Not that I thought Greyson would ever hurt me, but when I'd first met him and found out he was a vampire, there were a lot of unknowns. There were still some, frankly. And both men were bone-meltingly sexy. Cooper might not be dating anyone else, but Greyson very well could be. I'd be surprised if he wasn't, really.

And I was okay with that. I had to be. Because I wasn't about to give either of them up. I was so equally divided between the two that I wasn't sure I could ever choose one. And I hoped tonight's conversation with Greyson didn't go down that path.

Because if it did…well, I had no idea what lay at the end of that road.

Nor did I want to think about it any longer. I got up, tossed a frozen pizza into the oven (not even close to being as good as Salvatore's), then put on my standard B&E outfit. Kind of sad that I had a go-to outfit for criminal activities, but such was my life.

Black T-shirt, black yoga pants and, in deference to the August heat, black flip-flops. I watched a little TV while I ate my pizza and drank another Dr Pepper, then brushed my teeth, gathered my stuff and headed down to meet Birdie.

She was on time, which was nice, but her outfit wasn't even slightly ninja-esque. "Um, are you sure a hot pink pantsuit is the right choice for tonight's event?"

She gave me a quick once-over. "I can understand why you're dressed in black, but honey, it doesn't matter what I have on."

"It doesn't?"

"Nope."

"Can I ask why not?"

She smiled, and her eyes lit with that wolfy glow again. "Because I'm not going to look like this while I'm standing guard. That wouldn't be smart. People know me. But they don't know my wolf form, and in the dark, they'll just think I'm a German shepherd or some such creature. Best camouflage you could ask for."

"All right, then." Birdie just got more and more interesting. "We should get going, then. Has she left the house already?"

"She should have, but we'll know for sure when we get there." She pointed at a shiny, navy Mercedes. "That's me right there. Hop in."

I got in and waited until she was in the driver's seat. The car was pristine inside. "Will people know your car too?"

"Some, yes." She angled away from the curb and headed toward Francine's. "But I've already worked that out."

"How so? Are you going to park a few blocks away?"

She smiled. "Something like that."

The driveway she pulled into belonged to a lovely Victorian in the same neighborhood as Francine's house. There was another Mercedes in the driveway and lights on inside. "Someone lives here."

"Several someones." She tucked her purse into the backseat, then opened her door, got out and ducked her head in to speak to me. "Leave your purse here and come on."

I threw my bag in the back too, then followed her up the steps of the beautiful house. It was gorgeous and looked freshly painted. Whoever lived here took real pride in ownership.

Birdie knocked on the door.

A petite redhead answered. "Hey, Birdie."

"Good evening, Pandora." Birdie gestured at me. "This is my friend, Jayne Frost. Jayne, this is

Pandora Williams, the number one realtor in Nocturne Falls and a mighty fine witch to boot. She's one of Corette's daughters." Then Birdie whispered to Pandora, "She's the princess."

"Oh, yes, of course." Pandora stuck her hand out. "Nice to meet you, Jayne. Any friend of Birdie's is a friend of ours."

I shook her hand, still not clear what this was all about. I wasn't sure how close we were to Francine's. Maybe Pandora was going to use her witch skills to make the car invisible. "Nice to meet you too. Your house is beautiful."

"Thanks. It's really my boyfriend's place. It's still a little bit of a project, but we're getting there." She grinned. "Come on in."

I hesitated. "We kind of need to be somewhere."

Birdie grabbed my elbow and moved me toward the door. "This is all part of the plan, Jayne. You'll see."

Hoping for the best, but having my doubts, I went along. The house was equally impressive inside, even with the ladder in the hallway and the partially painted dining room.

Pandora led us through to the kitchen. "Cole and Kaley are at the movie in the park. Then they'll get ice cream after, so they won't be back for another hour or so."

"Perfect timing," Birdie said as we came to a stop.

"Perfect timing for what?" I asked.

"To leave the car here," Birdie said.

Pandora jerked her thumb toward the doors that led out to her porch. "Our house is right behind Francine's. You can cut through my backyard to get to her place, and no one will see you. Our backyard is a little overgrown, but nothing like it used to be. The upside to that is it makes great cover."

A shiver of panic went through me. This was not good. "You know why we're here?"

She put her hands up. "I do. But don't worry, I'm on your side."

That didn't matter. What we—what *I* was about to do was still technically illegal. The fewer people who knew about it, the better.

Birdie put her hand on my arm. "Jayne, you can trust Pandora."

Pandora nodded. "You can, I promise. I helped my mom with the visibility spell. I've done some research on imps since finding out that's what's behind all the craziness in town and they can be dangerous if directed. I definitely believe whoever wanted this imp in the first place meant to use it against someone."

I took a breath, feeling slightly better. "I agree and I think whoever wanted it will probably seek out other means to accomplish whatever the imp was supposed to."

"Me, too," Pandora said. "So get over there, get her client list and let's put an end to this."

"Okay." I looked at Birdie. "You ready?"

"Most definitely." She glanced at Pandora. "Thanks."

"You got it. But first…" She raised her hands and wiggled her fingers at us while speaking a few words in Latin. Then she grinned. "Just a little protection spell."

That made the last of my nerves go away. "Cool. Thanks!"

"Sure thing." She opened the French doors onto the porch and out Birdie and I went into the sprawling, overgrown garden of a backyard.

It must have really been something in its prime, and judging by the work that had already been done to the house, the yard would be returned to that state soon. We stopped halfway down a flagstone path that led to a dry fountain that looked like it had recently been cleaned out. Weeds and grass sprouted from every viable space, and here and there I could make out topiaries whose shapes were only discernible through hard squinting and a vivid imagination.

"This place was really something once, but Cole and Pandora will get it there again," Birdie said. "Now just give me a sec…"

I ran my finger along the edge of the marble fountain and thought of home. "The only gardens we have in the North Pole are indoor ones, but my mother's greenhouse is one of her favorite places." I looked beyond the yard to the house on the other side of a line of tall, narrow pines that divided the two properties. I couldn't see much of the house, but it seemed dark. "Are you going to shift now or when we get there?"

A soft woof answered me.

I turned to see a large gray wolf at my side. Instinctually I stepped back. "Birdie? I mean, who else, right? But wow. That was fast."

The wolf nodded.

This was weird. "I guess you can understand me?"

Another nod.

"But you can't speak? Or can you?"

A shake of the head this time.

Yeah, this was weird. Maybe more than weird. I was talking to a wolf, who was actually a slightly older-than-middle-aged woman who'd just been wearing a hot pink pantsuit two seconds ago. "So do your clothes become your fur or…"

She nodded again.

I shrugged. This was my life now. "Okay. You're still going to howl if anyone comes, right?"

She nodded.

"All right, let's go." Birdie trotted alongside me as I hiked through the brush to the line of trees. We paused there so I could take one more look at the house. Seemed quiet. "Okay. I'm going to enter through that back door on her porch."

Birdie woofed out a breath in acknowledgment.

I squeezed between the trees, and she followed, then veered off toward the side of the house. I kept going to the porch. I put my back against the door and listened, but there was nothing to hear, just the ambient sounds of the evening. Insects, distant cars, and somewhere, maybe at a neighbor's, a television.

Which meant that while Francine wasn't home, her neighbors were. I needed to be careful about letting light shine through the windows.

I tipped my head back and rolled my shoulders. Time to get moving. I channeled my magic and slipped under the door. The usual wave of nausea hit me, so I stayed still as I re-materialized.

Much like at Pandora's house, the back door joined the kitchen. Except Francine's kitchen was empty. The glass-front cabinets were bare of dishes and the counters uncluttered, except for a single cup next to a small coffeemaker and a slim stack of paper plates. A box of plastic utensils sat nearby.

Something about the loneliness of it all made me a little sad. But that didn't mean I was turning back. Francine was responsible for that imp being in town, and a citizen of Nocturne Falls might be in danger. That was enough for me to keep going.

The dim light coming through the windows

wasn't enough to make out the details I needed, so I pulled my phone out of my bra, where I'd tucked it earlier, and brought up my flashlight app.

I kept the light aimed low and in front of me as I started my search. This was my third time inside the house, but in the dark, with towers of boxes and most of the remaining furniture draped for moving, there was a distinctly creepy vibe to the place.

Didn't help that I wasn't supposed to be here.

I scanned the boxes, looking for anything marked *office* or *important*, but they all just said things like *kitchen*, *dining room*, *bath*. It made sense that what I was looking for wouldn't be boxed up yet. Not if Francine was still actively doing business, which Birdie had proven with her fake meeting stunt. Birdie had also proven that Francine was willing to deal in black market goods.

That alone made me more suspect of her than ever.

My gut said get upstairs. Chances were very good that's where Francine kept her essential documents. Possibly in a briefcase or on her laptop—but since I'd gotten a paper receipt from the moving company and Bryn had made such a big deal about accidentally giving me both copies, I was guessing that Francine liked to do things the old-fashioned way. On paper.

A lot of supernaturals did. Especially those who

dealt in things that fell, as Corette had put it, into a gray area.

I climbed the steps to the second story, cringing every time one of them creaked. Francine's bedroom wasn't hard to find. It was the only room that looked lived in. From the doorway, I could see that the bed, an elaborate brass thing with a tea rose patterned chenille spread, was neatly made.

White wood furniture finished out the rest of the bedroom set. Her dresser held a few things, some jewelry and a single crystal perfume bottle on a mirrored tray, a folded silk scarf and a hairbrush. Boring stuff.

I stepped inside and shifted my phone to light more of the room. There was no briefcase or laptop anywhere I could see.

Then an awful thought occurred to me. What if she'd taken everything with her to the fake meeting? Son of a nutcracker. I did another quick sweep of the room. Nothing. But then something pulled me back to her nightstand.

I went closer and brought my light up. The small bedside table held only a lamp and a book (*Winterbottom's Guide to Curious Antiques*), but the nightstand had a drawer. I crossed my fingers and slid it open.

I sucked in a breath. Inside was a ledger. I tucked the phone between my chin and chest and took the book out. Scribbled on the first page was a list of dates, names and items.

This had to be it, and frankly, it was a Christmas miracle that I'd found exactly what I was looking for so fast. I thanked my lucky stars.

I put the book on the bed and brought up my camera to take pictures of the pages.

Which was exactly when a low, keening howl pierced the quiet.

No longer caring about the flash, I snapped as many pics as I could as fast as possible and hoped the light couldn't be seen by whoever was approaching. I wasn't even sure the pictures were in focus, especially because my hands were shaking, but I did the best I could. I flipped page after page, then hit one that was blank. The next few were empty, too. Excellent. I hoped that meant I'd gotten everything.

I jammed the book back into the drawer and shut it, then hustled downstairs, careful not to trip over anything in the dark since turning my flashlight back on didn't seem like a smart move. Yeah, I know, neither did breaking into someone's house, but that gift had already been unwrapped.

I tucked my phone into my bra and went out the back door the same way I'd come in, desperate to leave before whoever Birdie had warned me about showed up. That meant I had to recover from the Saint Nick Slide while moving.

Which also meant I tripped down the stairs and landed in the grass at the bottom of the steps.

Instead of getting up, I took a moment and closed eyes in an attempt to stop things from spinning. Also, throwing up in Francine's yard would definitely leave some DNA behind. A few breaths later, when I no longer felt like I was on the deck of a ship in a violent storm, I opened my eyes. And stared directly at a pair of polished black boots.

Next to those were Birdie's sensible white driving mocs.

I lifted my head. Oh boy.

Sheriff Hank Merrow stared down at me, one hand on his gun belt. There was enough light to tell that he wasn't happy. Although he sort of wore that grumpy expression all the time, so it was difficult to judge his actual state of mind.

Birdie put her hand on his arm. "I told you, Hank, she was just having a look through the windows to see the house. It's my fault. I'm the one who told her the house was for sale."

He grunted. "The house has been sold for a month, Birdie."

Her eyes went innocently wide. "Oh no, I heard the deal fell through. That it was going back on the market. In fact, I parked at Pandora's so that we could go talk to her afterwards if Jayne liked the place."

He looked at me again. "Is that right, Miss Frost?"

Was lying to the police a crime? Probably, but I nodded anyway. Birdie's lie was a good one, and since I had nothing better to offer, going along seemed like the right plan.

He reached a hand down to me and helped me up. "You always go house hunting dressed like a cat burglar?"

"I, uh—" I cleared my throat and tried to buy myself some time by brushing the grass off my yoga pants.

"Hank, leave the girl be. What she's wearing is no concern of yours. I mean, honestly. If she was going to bust into someone's house, would she be wearing those silly shoes? They're hardly shoes at all. Certainly not appropriate for nefarious activities. More for a day at the beach if you ask me."

He slanted his eyes at her. "I didn't."

But that didn't stop her. "And really, to even accuse her of such a thing. She's royalty, for Pete's sake. My word, you could cause an international supernatural incident with these silly suppositions."

He frowned. "Birdie, I hardly think—"

"You want to explain to Charlie why Princess Jayne's uncle, *Santa Claus*, no longer delivers to Nocturne Falls? Well, do you?"

I raised my eyebrows like I was very interested in that answer too. In truth, I was trying very hard not to laugh. Birdie on a roll was an incredible thing to behold.

A moment passed before the sheriff spoke to me again. "You're still trespassing on private property. Whether or not the house is for sale makes no difference, you understand?"

"Absolutely. Won't happen again." I put on my most sincere face. I was good at looking contrite. Just ask my dad. "I'm really sorry. I certainly didn't mean to cause any trouble."

He nodded. "Go home. The two of you."

"Fine," Birdie sniffed. "Come on, Jayne. We might as well cut through here to Pandora's. It's just on the other side of these trees."

I brushed off a few more bits of grass as we started forward. I was amazed we weren't getting arrested. I didn't know if it was Pandora's protection spell or Birdie's persuasiveness, but I wasn't about to press my luck to find out.

Birdie shook her head as we reached the tree line. "Breaking and entering, my foot." She snorted and shot Hank a last look. "I will be five minutes late tomorrow. Now that I know you're given to jumping to conclusions, I thought I ought to tell you in case you decide I've been kidnapped or sold into slavery or some such thing."

"If only," he muttered.

"I heard that," she barked back.

I kept my mouth shut until we were back inside Pandora's house. That might have been the first time I remembered to breathe, too. I gulped down air, the feeling that I'd been holding my breath very real. "Yelping yetis, that was close."

Pandora locked the door and closed the curtains behind us. "What happened? I know something happened. I felt it."

"Mind if I sit?" I didn't wait for her to answer, just slumped into one of the chairs at the kitchen table.

Pandora bit her lip. "That bad?"

Birdie waved her hand through the air with the casualness of someone who'd just come from a leisurely evening stroll. "Oh, Hank showed up. I think he was following me. He always was a nosy child. I took care of it."

Pandora squinted like she was sure there was more to that story. "Well, I'm glad you didn't get into any trouble." She looked at me. "Did you find what you were after?"

"I think so, but I won't know for sure until I look at the pictures on my phone."

As if on cue, Pandora's cell chirped. She pulled the phone from her back pocket and typed something in response. Then she tucked it away. "Cole and Kaley are on their way home, so if you don't want to explain why you're here, you'd better go. I did ask him to bring me a pint of mint chip, though. That'll buy you a little time."

"Thank you." I stood. I was ready to be home. "I really appreciate the help. And the protection spell, which I'm sure gave Birdie the edge with the sheriff."

Pandora laughed. "I doubt that's true, but you're welcome all the same. Let me know if there's anything else I can do."

"I will."

Birdie and I headed out, and by the time we reached the warehouse, my pulse had finally returned to normal. She pulled alongside the curb and put the car in park. "Let me know what you find out from those pictures. I can run any names you come up with and tell you if they live in town or not."

"I'll probably just send them to you. I'll go through them tonight before I go to bed—there's no way I could sleep right now anyway—but I don't know enough people to know who lives here and who doesn't." I shook my head. "Thanks for coming with me."

She grinned. "It was fun."

"Maybe for you. I felt like my heart was going to beat out of my chest. We could have ended up in jail!"

She laughed. "Oh honey, Hank wouldn't arrest either one of us. I'm his aunt and you're royalty. He's much smarter than that."

"Good thing." He was clearly a man of the law, first and foremost, but tangling with his aunt was obviously something he preferred to avoid. "I'll let you know what I find. Have a good night."

"You too, Princess."

I grabbed my purse and got out, too weary to remind her to call me Jayne. I stumbled up to my apartment and was fishing for my key when I remembered that barging in could scare the imp away if he was in the box eating the fudge.

I kind of wanted to cry. After the night I'd had, I was not in the mood to slide under another door.

Sadly, I really didn't have a choice if I wanted to catch that stupid thing. I stood there for a moment, gathering my courage and giving myself a little pep talk, then finally did the deed.

I managed to quietly get into a seated position on the other side, giving myself a chance to recover close to the ground. I sat there for a good seven or eight minutes, eyes closed, just letting everything even out. Finally, I took my flip-flops off, set them by the door, and pushed to my feet.

I tiptoed over to the box.

An edge of the fudge was gone.

I held my breath and peered closer. There were tiny teeth marks and a little green dust in the box, but it was otherwise empty. The imp had been here. But if Corette's visibility spell was working, he certainly wasn't here now.

Snowballs.

Maybe he was still in the apartment. If so, I should shut the window first, then have a look around. I padded toward the window and immediately stepped in something squishy.

I closed my eyes. *Please don't let it be imp poop. Or worse, the imp.*

Lip curled, I lifted my foot for inspection. The ball of my foot was sticky with a creamy substance that smelled of nutmeg. Whew. Just my aunt's fudge. Then I got a tiny bit riled. That little bugger had taken a bite and spit it out!

Wow. He was going to be a tough customer if my aunt's fudge wasn't to his liking. I scraped the fudge off my foot with my fingernail, then got the window shut. I washed my hands before searching the apartment for the imp.

I didn't see it or green dust anywhere. Spider was sleeping in the bathroom sink. I nudged him. "Hey."

He yawned, then curled up harder, giving me a little meow. "Sleepy."

"I see that, but I need to ask you a question."

He smacked his lips. "Hungry."

"What's new? Listen, did you see a little green thing flying around the apartment tonight?"

He blinked up at me, suddenly interested. "Bug?"

"No, not a bug exactly. An imp. The thing that

you let out of the box when you knocked it over, but now it's supposed to be visible." I flapped my hands. Because why not imitate a creature I'd never seen? "It's green, or at least part of it is, and it flies around. Maybe looking for food. Anything?"

"Toy?"

I sighed. "I'll get you some dinner."

On my way to the kitchen, my left boob vibrated. I took my phone out and checked the screen. I had a text from Greyson.

Nightcap? Or are you still out?

I thought about it. I was pretty beat and really needed to go through those snaps I'd taken before bed, but seeing him would be great. And he knew everything that was going on, so maybe he'd have some idea about what bait to try in the box next.

Nope, just got home, I typed back. *Come on over.* Then I got to work getting Spider some food.

I kid you not, two minutes later Greyson was rapping on my window. I wasn't even done washing the Mackerel Stew off my hands. I turned the faucet off and grabbed a towel to dry with as I leaned back and glanced toward the window. "It's open."

He slid the window up and climbed through, his long legs first, then the rest of him following under like a limbo contestant. "Open or closed?"

"Open a crack. Thanks." I folded the towel and left it by the sink.

"Still haven't caught that imp, hmm?"

"Nope." I walked over to him, suddenly craving the comfort of his arms. "And apparently my aunt's fudge wasn't to his liking, so I have to come up with something new for bait."

He wrapped me in an embrace, his delicious, cinnamon scent making me realize my frozen pizza dinner hadn't really satisfied my hunger. He kissed me, soft and slow, then broke it off to smile down at me. "I'd think you're sweet enough on your own to draw him in."

I slid my arms around his neck. "You're just what I needed right now, you know that?"

His brows lifted. "Is that so? Well, I do like to pride myself on being where my woman needs me, when my woman needs me."

And there it was. The perfect segue. "Is that what you consider me? Your woman?"

His gaze narrowed a little. "I do not know the correct answer to that, and yet, I feel as though I should."

I sighed as I released him. Maybe it was just because I was tired, but I wasn't exactly sure how to ask the question I needed to. At least, I couldn't quite form the thought into a sentence that sounded more inquisitive than accusatory.

"Just say it, Jayne. You're not going to hurt my feelings." He looked like he was bracing himself for a letdown.

I had no idea what he thought was coming. He didn't think I was breaking up with him, did he? "I'd just like to know if you're seeing other women besides me. And there's no right or wrong answer. I just want to know."

His gaze stayed tapered. "I was seeing someone else, but that ended a month ago. It's just you now."

"Does it bother you that I'm still seeing Cooper?"

He shook his head slowly. "I'm not crazy about it. But I knew what I was getting into when we started going out." He relaxed a bit. "What's this about exactly?"

I raked my hair out of my face. "Cooper and I had a talk, and it got me thinking. I'm seeing both of you, but you're both just seeing me. It's not exactly a balanced situation."

"We're grown men, Jayne. Whatever choices we make are ours to make. And while you might think the situation is unfair, we're willingly a part of it." He shrugged. "You shouldn't let that weigh on you."

"You're sure?"

"Positive."

"Huh. You two sure are chill about all this."

He grinned. "You're worth it. At least as far as I'm concerned. And if I start to feel differently, I'll let you know."

"I appreciate that."

He shrugged. "Hey, I get you wanting to see if there's anything left of your college romance. Who wouldn't be curious about that? But I also know that you and I have something that can only be described as chemistry."

He wound a strand of my hair around his finger as he nuzzled the side of my neck. "And chemistry trumps history in my book."

I shivered from the touch of his breath on my skin, momentarily at a loss for words.

He feathered little kisses down to my throat, and my head went a little spinny while the rest of me warmed into a gooey mess. Then my stomach growled, confirming that my blood sugar might have been a bit low.

He laughed. "Need a snack, do you?"

"Dinner was a long time ago. And I've had a strenuous evening."

He tucked a stray strand behind my ear. "What are you in the mood for?"

Irish vampire, but that answer was going to lead us down a very different path. "Something sweet."

"I know just the thing." He smirked. "Trust me?"

"Of course." Then I held up a finger. "Does this require leaving the apartment?"

"Yes, but we won't be gone too long. Is that okay?"

"It's perfect. I just want to change into something less cat burglar and more upstanding citizen. Be right back." I ditched the yoga pants in favor of my jean shorts and was back at his side, flip-flops on and ready to roll. Sure, I still needed to go through those pictures, but my body needed fuel. "So. Where to?"

"You'll see. Fire escape or elevator?"

"Oh, I get a choice, do I?"

He laughed. "You always have a choice."

"I've had enough excitement for one evening. Let's take the elevator. But first I need to bait that box."

"Can I help?"

"Nope. It'll just take me a second." I grabbed the bottle cap and rinsed out the hunk of fudge, then filled it with one of the samples Delaney had sent. Molasses. No clue if it would work, but something had to. I glanced at the window, even though I already knew it was open. Everything was set. I tucked my phone into my purse. "All right, let's go."

He peeked into the box as we walked to the door. "You think that'll work?"

I shrugged. "Who knows? It's only the third thing I've tried, but this imp is proving tricky." I locked the door behind us and put my keys back in my purse.

He took my hand. "You'll get him."

"If only it wasn't taking so long."

"I know." He pushed the call button. "What did you do this evening? You said it was strenuous. I admit that's not how I picture a girls' night out."

I laughed sharply at his description. "Yeah, that's not really the kind of night I had." The elevator door opened. I stepped on. "I'll explain on the way down."

"You have to be more careful." Greyson's gaze took on a concerned light as we stepped off the elevator and into the warehouse. "The sheriff absolutely knew what you were doing. It was only because of Birdie that he didn't arrest you."

"I'm sure you're right. But you would have bailed me out, wouldn't you?"

"Of course." He squeezed my hand. "But just promise me you'll be more careful next time."

"I don't plan on there being a next time. And I thought I was being careful."

"With Birdie as your lookout?" He sighed. "I know she means well, but..."

"I didn't really see any other options."

He tugged me closer. "You could have called me."

My brows shot up. "Are you saying you want to be my partner in crime?"

"Can you think of anyone better?"

I couldn't. I kissed him. Short and sweet. "Next time, you're first on my list."

He smiled. "Good."

He led me down Main to a shop called I Scream. I'd been by it, but had yet to stop in. With my addiction to Delaney's running rampant, ice cream hadn't been much of a draw. Sure, I loved ice cream. Frozen treats were kind of a staple in the NP, and because ice cream was so common there (and magically delicious), Delaney's shop held more appeal to me.

He held the door for me. "Prepare yourself."

I cut my eyes at him. "For ice cream? Color me skeptical."

"You'll see."

The place was fairly busy, but most people were getting cones to walk with, so a lot of the tables were open. I stared up at the menu board. They had some interesting flavors, I'd give them that. I'd never seen buttered popcorn, bacon brittle, or smoked vanilla anywhere else. And then I noticed they had a whole board of adult flavors that all included alcohol. This place was growing on me.

He nudged me. "They make everything in-house."

"Even better. Any suggestions for what I should order?"

He stood hip to hip with me, looking up at the board. "How hungry are you?"

"Hungry. And you know how I feel about dessert-category offerings."

He grinned. "Get the Big Scream. It's not as large as the Scream Queen, but that one really ought to be shared."

I glanced at him. "You don't want to share with me?"

"I don't want to get in the way of your enjoyment. Also, the Scream Queen is generally recommended for parties of six or more. The Tower of Doom is slightly smaller, but it's still only four scoops less."

"Yeah, those both might melt before I can finish them. The Big Scream it is." I stepped up to the counter and placed my order, going mostly in a chocolate direction while including a few of the crazier flavors just for fun.

Greyson ordered his—a rather sedate sundae of Irish coffee ice cream, hot fudge and candied hazelnuts, then we took a little number on a stand so the server could find us when our order was ready, and picked out a table.

I pulled napkins out of the dispenser on the table and slid one over to him. "You want to help me look through the pics I took when we get back? Maybe see if you recognize any of the names?"

"Happy to. You really think it was someone in town and not one of her mail-order clients?"

"If it was a mail-order client, why have the imp delivered here and not directly to them? I don't know for sure, but my gut feels like there's more to this than she's saying."

"I believe that too. And at this point, anything more we can learn about the imp might be useful."

"True. Mostly I just don't want anyone else to get hurt, you know? Especially if I can prevent it."

He nodded. "Agreed." He looked past my shoulder and grinned. "Here it comes."

Two servers approached our table. Two, because the sundaes were just that large. The woman carrying mine actually grunted when she set it down in front of me. Then she added a single spoon, which was sort of like offering someone on a cruise ship a solitary oar. "There you go. Enjoy!"

"Sweet fancy Christmas." I stared at the mountain of ice cream before me. I almost couldn't see Greyson across from me. The scoops of ice cream had been stacked pyramid style, then rivers of hot fudge, salted caramel and marshmallow sauce had been drizzled over them. A variety of cookies had been stuck into the crevices, and then the whole thing had been liberally doused in chocolate sprinkles. Of course, there was also whipped cream and a cherry, which had been dipped in chocolate, because why not?

Greyson peered around the frozen atrocity with a gleam in his eyes. "Told you."

My mouth watered. This was a North Pole-worthy sundae for sure. "Challenge accepted."

Half an hour later, I'd gotten through only half of it and I was full. Like, Christmas dinner full. I dropped my spoon in defeat. "That's all I've got in me."

"You did valiantly." He'd finished his sundae well before me.

"Don't tease."

"No, I'm serious. I have a brand new respect for you. Watching you eat that was actually a little sexy."

"You're an odd man."

"So I've been told." He wiped his mouth. "Ready to go?"

"Yes. But you may have to roll me."

He laughed. "The walk will do you good." He got up and tossed a few bills on the table for a tip.

I stood. "I'm sure you're right."

He took my hand again, and we headed back to my place, happily quiet until we were at the warehouse door.

"I'll have to go into the apartment first to see if the imp is there."

"I can check for you right now."

"You can?"

He nodded and jumped, landing on the fire

escape above us as silently as Spider. He looked through the window, then leaped over the railing to rejoin me on the sidewalk. "Nothing."

I sighed and unlocked the door.

"Maybe by morning," Greyson said.

I nodded, but I was losing hope. Right now, having those pictures to focus on was a good thing. As soon as we got into the apartment, I grabbed my laptop and settled onto the couch, Greyson comfortably beside me. Then I fired up my computer and opened the photos that had automatically upload to my cloud so we could see them on a larger screen.

We studied the first picture, which was remarkably clear considering how rushed I'd been in taking them. "Recognize anyone?"

He pointed to a couple of them. "All of these, but the dates are from three years ago. None of these would be the imp. Hmm. Three years ago. Means she's been running this mail-order business for a while. I wonder if Roger knew."

"Maybe she was putting money aside? Who knows? Let me scroll to the last pic." I went forward in the gallery until I got to the last one. "How about from this list?"

He stared at the screen, his eyes skimming the names. "No. Nothing."

"Hang on." I went back a page. "Any of these look familiar?"

More reading. Then he shook his head. "Looks like she kept her business strictly out of town in the last year."

"She might have had to, given her prickly reputation."

He nodded and sat back. "I don't know everyone in town. I could definitely be missing someone. You should still run these by Birdie."

"I was planning on emailing her the pics before I go to bed." I looked at the time. "Which I should do immediately, seeing as how it's almost midnight and I have work tomorrow."

He smiled. "Cue taken. Glad I got to see you tonight."

"I'm glad I got to see you too. And thanks for taking me for ice cream. That was epic." I put the laptop on the coffee table. "I really appreciate you letting me talk out the whole relationship thing, too. I don't want this to get weird, but promise me that if anything ever changes for you, as in how you feel about us, you'll tell me so we can discuss it."

"Promise." He stood and offered me a hand. "I'll take the door. Just in case the imp is hovering out by the window somewhere, waiting to devour the bait."

I took his hand and let him pull me up. "Very thoughtful of you."

He tugged me into his arms, then threaded his

fingers into my hair and kissed me hard. "See you soon, my darling Jayne."

I nodded. "Night, vampire."

He smiled and slipped out the door. I locked it behind him, the dreaminess of his kiss still filling my head.

That dreaminess remained until the next morning, when I woke up to discover the box was still imp-free. That put me in a chilly mood. In fact, I almost uttered a few choice words, but seeing as how Spider could talk now, I wasn't sure I wanted him picking up those sorts of things from me.

I grabbed a Dr Pepper from my never-ending supply and stood by the window, looking for any sign of the imp. There was a small green smudge on the outer sill, but that was it. Had he been here and turned his nose up at the molasses? That seemed the only logical answer.

So the molasses was a no-go. I sorted through the box Delaney had sent, trying to decide what to try next.

Maybe the woman was psychic, but as I was doing that, she called. I grabbed my phone as soon as I saw her name on the screen. "Hello?"

"Good morning, Jayne. It's Delaney. Am I calling too early? Hugh said I should at least wait until the store was open."

"No, it's fine. What can I do for you?"

"I'm dying to know if any of the samples worked."

I sighed. "Not yet."

She groaned. "Which ones have you tried?"

"Just the molasses so far."

"Was there any sign of the imp?"

"Just a smudge of green dust on the sill. Nothing like yesterday when he actually took a bite out of the fudge. Although I found that bite on the floor, so he obviously didn't care for it either."

Delaney gasped. "He spit out your aunt's eggnog fudge?"

"Yep."

"Blasphemy. But he did at least take a bite of that, which gives me an idea. Can you spare an hour this morning?"

"Will it help me catch the imp?"

"It might."

"I'll work it out. What time?"

"Not sure. I need to make a call first. Can I text you with the info?"

"Sure. And thanks for the help."

"You got it. Talk soon! Bye!"

"Bye." I hung up, curious about what Delaney was up to, but happy and willing to take any help offered. I took my Dr Pepper into the shower, deciding to get to work early to make up for the time I would need to take off.

Twenty minutes later, I had Spider fed, myself

clothed and made up and was in my office. Breakfast was fudge, cookies and the last remaining truffle from the box Delaney had brought yesterday. The evening crew had decimated the offerings, but I didn't begrudge them the snacks. They worked hard.

I popped that truffle into my mouth, then headed into the store to get the bank bag that Buttercup would have left in the drawer under the register. She was in charge of closing every night, and thankfully, she was meticulous about it.

The shop was so quiet. In another twenty minutes, it would be hopping, but right now, with the lights and music off, it had a serene feeling to it.

I took the bag back to my office and sat down to go through the receipts from yesterday. My phone chimed before I could start. It was a text from Delaney.

Pick you up at the store in half an hour?

Sure, I texted back. I couldn't wait to see what she had planned.

Great!

I put my phone aside and dug into the receipts. As usual, everything was in order. I wrote up the day's report, added it to the bank bag, then dropped it into the Santa's Bag to send it to headquarters.

As I walked back to my office, Juniper came

out of the elevator. "Hey, you're early," I said.

"I was about to say the same thing to you. What are you doing down here already?"

"I have to head out for about an hour today." I rolled my eyes. "It's imp-related."

She nodded. "No problem, we'll cover things. I take it that means the bugger is still at large?"

"Yep. So why are you here so early?"

"I'm going to Mummy's for cinnamon rolls."

"Rolls? Plural?" I grinned. "Did Pete stay over?"

She swatted my arm playfully. "No. I'm getting one for me and one for Kip."

"That's very nice of you." I waggled my brows. "So...does Pete know he has competition?"

She wrinkled her nose. "It's not like that."

"Maybe not for you, but how does Kip feel?"

"We're just friends and he knows that." She narrowed her eyes. "Now quit teasing me or I won't bring you one."

I held my hands up. "My lips are sealed. Thank you! If I'm gone when you get back, I'll eat it when I return."

I went back to my office and knocked a few more things off my daily to-do list before another text from Delaney arrived.

Stanhill and I are outside.

I grabbed my purse, locked my office and headed to the sidewalk. A sleek black sedan was parked and waiting.

The rear window buzzed down, and Delaney grinned at me. "Hop in."

But before I could take another step, Stanhill got out and opened the door for me. "Morning, Your Highness."

I smirked at him. "Morning, Stanhill."

He shut the door and got back behind the wheel. As he pulled away from the curb, I leaned toward Delaney. "Where are we going?"

"To see the woman who I think could be the answer to our imp troubles." She set a paper bag between us. Her shop name and logo were emblazoned on the side. "Salted caramel peach muffin?"

Was she actually unsure if I wanted one? Eager to answer, my stomach rumbled. "Absolutely, thanks."

She offered me a napkin. I took one, spread it on my lap, then pulled a muffin out of the bag and dug in. It was heaven. "This is so good," I mumbled around a mouthful. "That was really thoughtful of you to bring them."

"My pleasure. I might be a vampire, but I still believe there are very few occasions that can't be improved with something sweet."

My girl crush on her deepened. "Can we be best friends?"

She laughed, showing off her cute little fangs. "Happily." She took the second muffin out of the bag, and before long, we had them both polished off.

We put the wrappers and napkins in the bag as Stanhill turned onto a long gravel drive.

Delaney inched forward excitedly. "We're almost there."

I still had no idea where we were going, but we weren't in town anymore. Instead, countryside spread out around us. "Where are we exactly?"

Delaney nodded toward something beyond the window.

The car slowed, and I glanced that way to see for myself. A small cottage was up ahead, something that would have been right at home in the English countryside. Flowers of all kinds, even flowering bushes, were everywhere. And at the back of the property were rows of white boxes.

A sign outside the door read Matilda Sharpe, Mistress of Bees.

"Bees?" My brows knit as I looked at Delaney.

"Not just bees. Magical bees," she said. "And, more importantly, their honey." Then she bit her lip. "That is, if Matilda decides to share it with us. Which I'm sure she will. She basically said she would on the phone, but she wants to meet you first."

"Decides? She controls the bees?" And no pressure on me or anything.

Delaney bobbed her head. "Sort of."

"Is she a supernatural? A bee shifter or something?"

"Not a shifter, but sort of a magical bee whisperer. She can speak to the bees and has the ability to imbue magical properties into the things she produces with the honey and the wax. I'm hoping she can provide us with some spelled honey to lure the imp in and keep him in the box until you can get the lid closed."

"That would be great."

She smiled. "Let's go introduce you to Mattie, then."

Matilda Sharpe came around from the back of the cottage as we got out of the car. She was a woman of average height, above-average curves and the owner of an infectious smile. Her whiskey-brown eyes and matching twin braids made a pretty picture combined with the smattering of freckles across her cheeks. I'd never met a magical beekeeper before (who had?), but Matilda seemed to fit that description perfectly.

She wore an ivory apron over a long-sleeved, pink plaid shirt and denim shorts that showed off shapely tanned legs. The pockets of her apron held a few gardening tools, and the smudges of dirt on the fabric clearly said it wasn't just for looks. She wiped the hair out of her eyes with the back of her hand as she approached. She nodded to Delaney. "Hey."

Delaney nodded back. "Hi, Mattie."

She stopped in front of me, her gaze pointed and assessing. "You must be the winter elf who set the imp free."

"That's me, but it wasn't on purpose, I assure you."

A pair of bees buzzed past me. I held still as they landed on her shoulder. They weren't something I was familiar with, and in truth, they scared me a little. I didn't want to get stung.

Mattie didn't seem to have that concern, since she acted like they weren't even there. "Tell me again how it happened."

"How the imp got free? I bought the box from Francine Gresham's estate sale, brought it home, my cat knocked it off the coffee table and the lid popped free. I didn't even know there'd been anything in the box until all the nonsense in town started happening."

She nodded, then glanced at the bees and tipped her head at them. Like she was listening. Were they saying something?

I didn't hear a thing.

When the bees took off, she looked at me again. "The bees say you're telling the truth."

"They can tell?"

"Bees pick up on vibrations humans can't register. And I can understand the bees. It's my gift. Been in my family a long time."

"That's very cool. Does me telling the truth

mean you're going to give me some of your honey?"

She smiled. "Yes. But it'll take me a moment. I need to tell the bees the purpose of the honey first, then harvest it." She wiggled her fingers. "Work my magic, as it were."

A small swarm of bees flew overhead.

I ducked.

Mattie grinned. "Come on in the house, both of you. You can wait there."

We followed her. The cottage was just as cute inside as it was out and still just as English.

"Have a seat at the table there if you like." She pointed toward the small kitchen table covered with a floral cloth. "Can I get you anything?"

"I'm all right." I glanced at Delaney.

She shook her head. "All good here."

"Back in a bit, then. There's lemonade in the fridge if you get thirsty." She started for the door.

I had to ask. "Aren't you going to put on protective gear so you don't get stung?"

Mattie smiled. "My bees never sting me."

"Nice."

She left us, and Delaney settled back in a chair. "If this honey doesn't do the trick, I have no idea what to try next, but I have a feeling it'll work. Especially after your aunt's fudge showed so much promise."

I thought about that. "You think because that fudge was made by an elf—"

"Not just an elf," Delaney said. "But a very special one. Santa Claus's better half."

"So you think Mattie's magic honey might do the trick because it's also produced by a supernatural?"

"I do. It's got the whole supernatural element, but it's also of the earth. That deeper connection might just be the thing."

I took a breath. "I sure hope you're right." A few moments of silence passed. "How long have you known Mattie?"

"Not long. She just moved here a few months ago. She's a friend of the brother and sister who own the winery we passed. He was looking for help pollinating the vines, so he called her."

"I still don't think I understand what kind of supernatural she is."

"The most I can tell you is that she's an ancient kind of Celtic witch. A green witch, like Corette's daughter Marigold, but a very specific type that has this gift with bees. It's pretty rare, from what I know."

I looked around. "Celtic? That explains the house."

"Looks straight out of an English village, doesn't it?" Delaney smiled. "Hugh's grandmother loves it. She lives just down the road. I've heard her mention it at least three or four times since Mattie's been here."

"Well, the cottage didn't just magically appear when she arrived. Who built it?"

Delaney's brows rose. "Actually, it kind of did."

"Are you serious?"

"I told you she was a witch."

The cottage door opened, and Mattie came in holding a small Mason jar filled with liquid gold. She held it out to me. "I took a bit of the honeycomb, too. Use it. The wax holds a scent that should help draw the imp in."

I took the jar. It was warm and weighty, and I was instantly filled with hope. "Thank you so much."

Delaney hoisted herself upright. "If I weren't pregnant, I'd be asking for a couple bottles of your mead."

Mattie smiled. "As soon as the baby's born, I'll make you some."

"Mead is…" I looked at both of them.

"Wine made from honey," Mattie answered.

Delaney made a happy little sound. "Her mead really is magical. Sweet and delicious and just the best stuff I've ever tasted."

Sounded awesome.

Mattie bobbed her head. "Much appreciated. Same shipment of honey this week for the store?"

"Yep," Delaney said. "Those honey bourbon

truffles are a big hit. Or so I've heard." She patted her stomach. "One more thing this kidlet is keeping me from tasting."

"I'll be by with the jars as usual, then."

"Great," Delaney said. "I'll see you later. And thanks again for your help with this."

"Yes," I said. "Thank you. I have a good feeling that this honey is going to do the trick. One question...is it okay if I taste the honey? I mean, it won't hurt me, will it?"

Mattie laughed. "You can taste it all you like. Just leave enough for the imp."

"I promise."

We left Mattie's, and Stanhill, who'd read the paper in the car while he'd waited, drove us back to town. They dropped me off at the shop.

"Call me tomorrow," Delaney said. "I have to know if this works."

"Will do." I gave her a wave, the jar of honey snug in my other hand. As the car pulled away, I set the jar on the sidewalk to get my key out. That felt safer than fumbling around and risking dropping it.

Once in, I went straight upstairs and set up the box with the new bait. The honey smelled amazing as I dripped it into the bottle cap along with the little bit of wax I'd cut free with a knife. I couldn't resist having a little taste. Sweet and floral and utterly delicious. If the imp didn't like this, I might just have to take my dad up on his offer to freeze the whole town.

I went downstairs to check in at the shop and let Juniper and Kip know I'd returned, then I finally headed into my office. The entire space smelled of cinnamon, and I grinned at the Mummy's bag on my desk. That muffin had been great, but there was always room for a little cinnamon roll. Or a lot, in the case of Mummy's.

Then I frowned. I'd locked my office before I'd left. And Juniper had just told me that the cinnamon roll was in a bag in *front* of my door.

"Hello, beautiful."

I jumped and shrieked as I turned. Greyson stood against the far wall looking at some family photos on top of the filing cabinet.

He frowned. "Sorry. Didn't mean to startle you."

"How did you get in here?"

He shrugged. "You're not the only one good at breaking and entering. Which reminds me, that's a pretty basic lock on that door. You should upgrade it if you really want to keep whatever's in here secure."

I frowned right back. "I don't know how I feel about you breaking into my office."

He nodded. "Understood. But I didn't think you'd want me loitering outside either. I know I'm not Juniper's favorite supernatural. If I overstepped, I'm very sorry."

"No, it's okay." And it was. I trusted Greyson.

Just like I trusted Cooper. "And you're right. Juniper would have freaked if she'd walked into the warehouse and bumped into you."

"I wouldn't have done it, except I have some news."

That got my attention. "You do? About the imp?"

"Sort of. Your idea that Francine is hiding something got me thinking. After I left your place last night, I went by her house. And did a little investigating on my own."

"Investigating? What's that mean?"

He hesitated. "It means I went inside and had a look around."

"Greyson." I stared at him. "You just warned me about doing that."

"I realize the irony, but I'm a vampire. I'm much faster than you, and my skills allow me to be very stealthy."

"Apparently." I crossed my arms. "So what did you find out?"

"I'm not sure." He reached into his pocket and took out his phone. "I saw this in the butler's pantry off the kitchen. She's got all her shipping and packing supplies in there for the business. Her laptop was in there too, but I didn't even touch that."

"No wonder why I couldn't find that stuff."

He turned his phone so I could see a picture on the screen.

I squinted at it until I sort of understood what I was looking at. "A wooden crate?"

"A wooden crate *and* lid *and* the packing foam that was custom fit to whatever was originally shipped in that box. Look familiar?"

I peered at the picture again, then used my fingers on the screen to zoom in. The shape in the foam was about the size of the box upstairs. I glanced at him. "Is this the original packaging from the imp box?"

He nodded.

"Okay. But I don't get why this is news. I already know it was shipped to her. That's how she got it."

He swiped to the next picture. "But look who she was getting ready to send it to."

I glanced at the phone. There was no need to blow up the photo this time. The new label on the crate very clearly read Roger Gresham. The address was in Arizona, which was where Greyson had said he'd moved to.

I blinked, mulling that over. "I don't get it. Her husband ordered the imp? Why wouldn't he just buy it for himself? And why would she be doing him a favor when she must hate the guy?"

Greyson laughed and kissed me. "I love how sweet you are, Princess. Always thinking the best about people. Never change."

"What?"

"I doubt he knows anything about the imp. Look at the return address."

I checked the picture again. The return address listed Saul Zabarski as the sender. And he was apparently in Greensboro, North Carolina. "I don't know what to make of that."

Greyson clicked the phone off and put it away. "I do. Francine is Saul."

My mouth gaped as everything fell into place. "Of course. She's the one who wants revenge."

"And she's moving to Summerfield, North Carolina. Her sister lives there. Summerfield is right outside of Greensboro. It would be very easy to send a package from there and get the right postmark. For all we know, she's created this Saul character and used this alias to befriend Roger. He might even be expecting this package, thinking it's something else of course."

"Wow. She's craftier than I guessed."

He nodded. "Indeed. And think about how easy it would be to hurt someone with the imp. All you'd have to do is open the box, speak the control words to set your wishes in order with the imp, then seal it up again and send it on its way."

"With some kind of note that would get the recipient to open the box and release the imp, allowing it to fulfil those wishes." I looked at Greyson. "She could have wished for anything. For the imp to burn down Roger's house. Or for him to be covered in boils. Or for his you-know-what to fall off. That would be poetic. Considering."

Greyson's brows arched. "Yes, I suppose so. I was thinking more along the lines of she might ask the imp to destroy Roger's new marriage and business. Or worse."

"You think she would have wished for the imp to kill Roger?"

He shrugged. "She might have. Then she could have asked the imp to make his body disappear. It would be the perfect crime."

"Holy snowballs."

Greyson sat on the loveseat. "Pretty much."

I took the chair behind my desk. "But we can't prove any of this. And you can't exactly show the sheriff your pictures without explaining how you got them."

Greyson tipped his head. "Therein lies the dilemma."

I sat back. "We're going to have to handle this ourselves. If we can get her to confess, and we can record it, then that should be worth something."

"And how do you suppose you're going to get her to confess?"

I sighed. "I have no idea. But I'll come up with something."

"Better come up with it fast. Judging by the interior of her house, she's not going to be here much longer."

"One more day." I shrugged. "Birdie told me."

Then I squinted as a new thought popped into my head. "I wonder if there's a way to keep her in town a little longer…"

I showed up at Cooper's that evening after work in my tiniest sundress, strappy sandals, a push-up bra and full makeup and hair. I was also carrying two takeout orders of peach cobbler from Howler's and the DVD of Die Hard, which had been Coop's favorite movie in college. Basically, I'd turned myself into a package he couldn't resist.

Not that I thought there would be any resistance. He already knew I was coming over. He'd offered to make me dinner, and I'd said yes. Because for one, I felt like I needed some time with him after seeing Greyson unexpectedly, and for two, I was seriously hoping he might be able to help me with my problem.

There was also the whole Lark thing, but frankly, I'd be fine pushing that to the back burner and leaving it there. We'd also decided not to discuss the imp's latest rampage through town, which had included three side streets covered in yellow slime, a dog at one of the parks suddenly becoming the size of an elephant, and loud popping sounds that seemed to serve no other purpose than to scare people.

Cooper opened the door almost as soon as I started knocking.

I grinned up at him. "Hey, sailor."

I was rewarded with the right kind of look in his eyes. Desire. But then his gaze narrowed, and he shook his head. "I know I'm going to regret asking this, but what ulterior motive lies behind all"—he waved a finger at me—"this?"

I clutched my nonexistent pearls. "I'm wounded. And I just wanted to look nice for you."

"I appreciate that." He moved out of the way to let me in. "Especially since the last couple of times I've seen you, you were dressed to clean toilets."

"I was not."

"I meant *if* you cleaned toilets." He winked at me. "Hi." Then he kissed me. "I do appreciate the effort, whatever the reason. You look gorgeous. But then you always look gorgeous. Even when you're a bum."

I kissed him back. I couldn't argue, because he was right that I hadn't put in much effort before. "Thanks."

"Is that cobbler I smell?"

"Yep." I lifted the bag. "I said I'd bring dessert. What's for dinner?"

He answered as we walked into the kitchen. "Salmon with dill sauce, asparagus and roasted fingerling potatoes."

"Wow, fancy." The house smelled like dill and garlic and something else I couldn't name, but if the food tasted like the aromas floating in the air, it was going to be a fantastic meal. "I'm impressed."

He shrugged. "Firemen like to eat."

"Yeah, but you're doing more than that."

He seemed pleased with my praise. "Hey, I can cook."

I set the bag on the counter. "I can't. Not much beyond the basics anyway."

"That's because you had people to do it for you." He shot me a teasing glance, but it was a true statement that I once again had no argument for. "Wine?" he asked.

"Sure. If it's okay with you, could we not talk about Lark tonight? I know that's partially why I came over, but I'm just not in the mood."

"Fine by me." He poured us both a glass, then handed one to me and lifted his in a toast. "Thanks for coming over."

"Thanks for cooking. And cleaning up. You know, since I'm not dressed for it." I pursed my mouth to punctuate that statement before clinking my glass to his.

He laughed. "Touché."

We drank, and I felt better about having to ask him for help. This was Cooper, after all. He'd want to help me.

But dinner came and went, and before I knew it, we were side by side on the couch, opening credits rolling, and my question still unasked. He slipped his arm around my shoulders, and I settled in against him. His muscles were surprisingly comfy, but I couldn't stop thinking about the ticking clock of Francine's departure. I just hadn't found the exact right moment to bring up the subject.

He kissed my temple, then picked up the remote and hit pause. "You okay?"

I twisted to look at him. "Why do you ask?"

"You feel tense."

I hesitated.

He didn't. "What is it, Jay? What's bothering you?"

I sighed before answering. "It's the imp. More than that, really." I explained about how Francine was leaving and I still hadn't figured out everything I needed to. How I felt like she was about to get away with something. I kept the part about my and Greyson's *visits* to her house to myself. I knew there was only so much Cooper would let slide. I stuck to my original idea, before Greyson had discovered the shipping crate. "I'll catch the imp eventually, but whoever it was meant for could still be in danger. I feel like if I just had a little more time—"

"Would another twenty-four hours do it?"

I narrowed my eyes. "Sure, but how am I going to manage that?"

He smiled. "You won't. But I can."

"How?"

"Both the sheriff's office and the fire department have to sign off on the permits necessary for trucks that size to enter the town limits. I'll just find an error on the permit tomorrow and delay the process."

"You'd do that for me?"

"Absolutely. Would that help?"

"Tremendously. Thank you." Logically, I knew twenty-four hours wasn't that much longer, but at that moment, it felt like everything.

He leaned back a bit. "So is that what the outfit was for? To warm me up and put me in a helpful mood?"

Yes. But I wasn't admitting to that. "Helpful? Is that the mood this put you in?" I glanced down at myself. "This dress must be broken."

With a soft growl, he grabbed my hand and tugged me against him. I gave in. Happily. Cooper was a great kisser and we did a lot of that.

A lot.

Vertical kissing led to horizontal kissing, and things were really heating up when the movie suddenly came back on. We both jumped, and then I laughed as I reached under me and pulled the remote out from under my backside. "Pretty sure I did that."

He took it from me and set it on the coffee table, then leaned over me, one hand on either side of me. I gazed up at him. He was so pretty it made my heart hurt. Fire danced in his eyes. "Might be time to call it a night, because I don't think either one of us is ready to take the next step."

I was sure he was ready, but it was nice of him to say otherwise for my benefit. "Okay." Then I exhaled a long, slightly frustrated breath as he helped me up. "But the day's going to come when I am ready to take that next step." Soon, maybe.

His brows lifted. "Does that mean you're about to make a decision?"

"No. Just...ready to do more than make out like teenagers." The history that we had made it difficult not to think about doing more than just kissing. Because we'd already done more than kissing. And we knew how good it could be. I mean, if I was remembering our college escapades, he had to be thinking about them too.

He studied me. "You do that with me and I'm going to assume your choice has been made."

I looked at him. "Are you saying if I sleep with you then I should sleep with Greyson, too?"

"Hell, no. But...maybe. No, wait, what am I

saying?" He thought a second, then groaned. "I can't believe we're having this conversation. What are you doing to me, woman?"

I shrugged and got up, straightening my twisted dress. "If you don't think I'm worth it—"

He pulled me onto his lap. "I'm still here, aren't I?"

I smiled.

He kissed me once more. A soft, easy kiss that held none of the heat our earlier ones had. "Let's get you home."

He walked me back to the warehouse, which wasn't far since he lived in one of the town houses near the fire station, then he said good night and I was in the elevator, headed to my apartment.

At the door, I put my ear to it and listened. I had no idea what an imp eating honey would sound like. But silence greeted me. My only option was to slip under the door soundlessly or risk spooking the creature.

I slid under, doing the same thing I had last time and landing in a seated position. I took my shoes off and sat quietly until the dizziness passed. I could see the box on the table. It looked empty from here. But the imp could be inside, already asleep.

I got up and tiptoed over.

The box was empty and the honey untouched. I tried not to let that ruin my spirits, but I'd been so sure the honey would work. Maybe it still would.

I put a can of cat food out for Spider before he could start yowling about it and went to bed.

When daylight woke me the next morning, I didn't do a lot of moving. Instead, I lay there, staring at the ceiling. And not just because Spider was asleep on my hair. I had to figure out how to get Francine to confess. There had to be a way to trick her into it. Maybe Birdie could come up with something.

I had to talk to her about the list of names anyway. Might as well get her thoughts on coercing a confession out of someone.

I needed to tell Greyson that Cooper was going to buy us some more time with Francine, too, but I wanted to wait until I knew that was going to happen for sure.

Spider stirred, stretching and yawning right in my face.

"Nice breath."

"Spider hungry."

"Yep, I know the drill." I disentangled him, then got up and padded out to the box. The routine was actually becoming routine, just like my disappointment at seeing the stupid thing empty every morning.

I yawned as I neared the box. There was an odd sound in the living room. Like something electronic had been left on and was humming with power. I glanced around, but there was really only the TV and the cable box, and they were both off.

I ignored it and looked into the box. That's when the sound made perfect sense. It was snoring. From the imp now sleeping next to the empty bottle cap. It was about the size of a hummingbird and the same iridescent emerald green. Its wings were crystalline like a dragonfly and folded around its plump little body.

I froze in shock. For a few seconds I couldn't even remember what to do next. Then my brain kicked into gear. I grabbed the lid and carefully eased it into place. My hands were shaking with excitement, and I was holding my breath, but three seconds later, I'd done it.

The lid was on.

And the imp was in the box.

Merry freaking Christmas, the honey had worked! I wanted to dance and shriek and make it snow, but first I had to secure that lid. I could not risk the box being opened again.

I grabbed a couple of hair ties from the bathroom and slid them around the box. They were pretty tight being stretched that far. There was no way that lid could accidentally come off now.

Spider strolled out, still looking very sleepy.

"Spider, I caught the imp. I caught it!" I picked him up and whirled him around, singing a happy little nonsense song I made up on the spot. "The imp is in the box, the imp is in the box, hi ho the dairy-o, the imp is in the box."

He meowed. "No like, no like."

"Okay, sorry." I put him down and he wobbled toward his water dish.

He didn't quite make it before he yacked up a hairball.

"Way to take the shine off the moment." But nothing could dampen the way I was feeling. The madness was over. I grabbed some paper towels, cleaned up the mess, then sent out a group text to everyone I could think of, which was Greyson, Cooper, Delaney, Corette, Birdie, Juniper and Buttercup.

My phone blew up for the next fifteen minutes, and by the time I was done answering everyone, I really needed to get in the shower and get to work.

Jubilation amped up my speed, and I practically danced my way into readiness, my steps bouncy with joy and my heart helium-light. Knowing that I'd finally put the imp problem behind me made me feel like I'd saved the world.

I hadn't, of course, and I knew that, but I'd kind of saved my world. There'd be no more dirty looks or questioning glances from the locals, that was for sure. And no more awful events to feel guilty over.

Jupiter came in early, and we did some extra happy dancing in the warehouse. Then I gave her twenty bucks and sent her to Mummy's for a dozen cinnamon rolls with extra glaze. Why not? Wasn't every day I thwarted the effects of gray magic in my new hometown.

While she was out, I called my dad on the globe and filled him in. Life was good.

Better than good, it was grand.

It was *glorious*.

At least until Francine Gresham walked into my office.

Juniper walked in behind her. "This lady says she has an appointment with you."

Obviously, she didn't, but the fact she'd told Juniper that was certainly confirmation of Francine's propensity for lying. And since I wasn't about to pull Juni any deeper into this mess, I just nodded and said, "Thanks."

Juniper gave me a smile as she left and closed the door.

I glared at Francine. "What are you doing here?"

Her haughty gaze darkened. "You have something that belongs to me."

"Oh? What's that?"

"You know very well what I'm referring to."

"I really don't. I paid for everything I bought at the estate sale, so as far as I'm concerned, we're square." Did she really think I was going to give the imp back to her? Also, how fast did word travel in this town that two hours after I captured the thing, she was in my office?

She made a bored face. Like *I* was wasting *her* time. "I want the box back."

"Just the box?" I really wasn't interested in having a big, long conversation with her, but at the same time, keeping her here gave me a better chance of coming up with a way to make her confess.

"Miss Frost, your games don't amuse me. The box. Now."

If only I was recording this. I put my hand on my cell phone, but there was no way I could casually figure out how to video our conversation without her realizing what I was doing. I needed more time. "Are you prepared to refund the money I spent on it?"

That seemed to catch her off guard. "I suppose."

"Good, because if you want that box back—"

"You do know we're not just talking about an empty box, correct?"

I rolled my eyes. "Yes, I know that. And if you want it back, all of it, then I want my money refunded for everything I bought. *Everything*. And I'm not taking a check."

There was no way she had that much cash on her. At least I was hoping she didn't.

She snorted. "That's ridiculous."

I shrugged and started to fuss with the paperwork

on my desk. "You can see yourself out, then."

"Fine." The word came out from clenched teeth. "Bring me the box."

I raised a skeptical brow. "You have that much money on you right now?"

"Bring me the box, and I'll bring you the money."

"Hah! What kind of fool do you think I am? You're not getting the box until I see the cash." I stared at her. "How about I come by your house tonight after work? About nine. We can make the exchange then."

"I can't wait that long. You can bring it to my house in an hour."

"Yeah, unlike you I have an actual legal business to run. So it'll either be tonight after work or not at all." I needed time to set things up. "What's it going to be?"

Her eyes narrowed, and she seemed to be thinking it over.

"Look," I said. "I don't want that thing. At all. But I do want to be compensated for all the crap that happened and the ding to my reputation. So either pony up the dough, or I'm going to flush that little green monster right down the—"

"Tonight after work at my house." She sniffed. "If you're a minute past nine, the deal is off."

I let the tiniest, smug smile creep onto my face. "No, it won't be. We both know that. But I won't be late."

I also wouldn't be alone.

I called Greyson and figured out pretty quickly that he wasn't happy with my plan. The displeasure was plain in his voice. "There's too much risk. You should let me do it."

I hoped he'd still go along if he couldn't come up with anything better. "She's expecting me. I'm not sure she'd let you in. Not after your last encounter with her."

"I suppose you're right." He sighed.

"Look, it'll be all you once I get us inside. I'll just step back and let you do your interrogation thing. Cool?"

"I guess. But it would be better if you weren't a part of it at all. That way, if she was to say anything about it later, you'd be blameless."

"She's not going to say anything."

"She will if this results in some kind of punishment. She'll say she was coerced. That we pressured her into confessing with cruel and unusual means. That it was supernatural against human. The magical courts don't look favorably upon that, you know."

"First of all, that's why we're going to video the whole thing. As proof that all we did was talk. You can handle that, right?"

"Yes, I have that covered. Francine will have no idea."

"Good. Secondly, what magical court would this

go to? Because I can't see this getting sent up to the North Pole."

"I imagine they'll convene a council right here in Nocturne Falls. Deal with it in-house, as it were." He paused. "Speaking of, I imagine you already called the fireman?"

I grimaced, thankful he couldn't see me over the phone. "No." I'd wanted to include Cooper, but I didn't want to get him in trouble by association. I imagined a fireman could lose his job for what we were about to do. Plus, I knew he'd want to get the sheriff in on it, and that just wasn't going to end with the result I needed.

"Probably better," Greyson said. "And I don't mean that for any reason other than this could jeopardize his job. As much as I consider him my rival in all things Jayne, there are certainly far worse choices you could have made."

"That's what I was thinking. About not getting him involved, I mean." It was nice to hear Greyson say that about Cooper. It made me feel better about both of them.

"You realize this makes us partners in crime," Greyson said. "Literally."

"Just so long as we don't end up sharing a jail cell."

"You wouldn't share a cell with me?"

"I'm sure it would be great fun until you got hungry."

A groan of disbelief left him. "You really think I would do that to you?"

"Wouldn't it get to a point where your hunger left you no choice?"

"Perhaps. But that would take a long time." He made a small, perturbed noise. "I'm not an animal."

I made the same noise right back at him. "Well, I don't know how these things work. We've never really talked about it."

"You're right. We haven't." His tone softened. "How about we do that? I'll answer whatever questions you have. At this stage in our relationship, you shouldn't be wondering about those sorts of things."

"Okay. And thank you. But first, Francine."

"Yes. Absolutely. I'll meet you at your place at eight thirty. Unless you want me to come sooner? Maybe bring some Salvatore's?"

"That sounds awesome, but I'm not sure I'll be able to eat. I might be too nervous."

He laughed. "Lass, I adore you, but I cannot imagine you too *anything* not to eat Salvatore's."

"No, you're probably right. Come over at seven. With pizza."

"You got it. See you then." He hung up and so did I.

I stared at my desk for a moment, thinking about what lay ahead. It wasn't going to be an easy night. But it had to be done. I kind of spaced out for a moment, which was why I didn't immediately see the snow churning in the globe.

I grabbed it and pushed the button.

My mom's face showed up. "Hi, honey. How are you?"

It was really nice to see her. "I'm good. How are you?"

"I'm just fine. Dad said you called earlier. I'm sorry I missed you."

"I'm sure he told you I caught the imp."

"He did. That's great news. Good job."

"Thanks." I waited expectantly. "Everything okay or did you just call to congratulate me?"

"That, but also Dad said you wanted to talk to Aunt Martha. I've got her with me."

My aunt stuck her head into view and waved. "Hi, Jaynie."

"Hi, Aunt Martha. Thank you for the fudge. It's been a big hit." I didn't bother telling her the imp hadn't cared for it.

"Oh good, I'm so glad. Would you like some more?"

"I'd love some. And that's kind of what I wanted to talk to you about. My friend Delaney, she runs the sweet shop here in town, well, I gave her a piece of your fudge, and she just about lost her mind over it. She said she'd never tasted anything like it and begged me to ask you if you'd be willing to work out some kind of a deal that would allow her to sell it in her shop for the holidays. Also, she gave me explicit instructions to tell you that she's pregnant and the fudge would make the baby happy."

Aunt Martha laughed. "Your friend sounds like a hoot. I'm tickled she liked it. But I can't give away that recipe."

My mother rolled her eyes. "Even I don't have that recipe."

"I'm aware. But maybe you could make the fudge and send it here through the Santa's Bag? I mean, she could purchase it from you for whatever price the two of you work out. You could put the money towards..." I shrugged. My aunt didn't need the money, so I wasn't really sure what she'd use it for.

"Ooo..." Her eyes lit up. "I could finally buy myself that Bosch oscillating power saw. It's got a universal adapter plate, you know."

I didn't, actually. I wasn't even sure what a Bosch oscillating power saw was. Besides a saw, obviously. That oscillated. Did I mention my aunt had a thing for woodworking? "Why haven't you bought it for yourself already?"

"Well, I have one. But it's not a Bosch."

"I see."

"No, you don't. You're giving me the same look your uncle does when I mentioned getting a new piece for my collection." She waved her hand. "Every time I order a new tool, your uncle gives me the business about it. Says I have enough already. But how else am I supposed to get my projects done?"

I shook my head like I completely sympathized. "What are you working on right now?"

She smiled brightly. "I'm building a new coat rack for one of the employee lounges in the stuffed-animal division."

"That's very kind of you. I'm sure they'll love it." I gently steered the conversation back to the fudge. "Does that mean you'll make a few batches for her this December?"

She pushed her wire-rimmed glasses back and squinted at me. "I'll think about it. Give me a day or two, all right?"

"All right. Thank you. I love you both, but now I must get back to work."

"You're so industrious," my mother crowed.

Hah. If only she knew how much time off I'd taken because of this imp.

They waved good-bye. "Love you!"

"Love you too." I pushed the button and disconnected the call.

Then my cell phone rang. I answered. "Hi, Birdie. What's up?"

"You're not going to believe this," she whispered.

She must have been at the sheriff's department and didn't want anyone to overhear. "What is it?"

"I took the liberty of checking into Francine's accounts—"

"Okay." Was that legal? I didn't want to know.

"She wired a large sum of money to someone in the Ukraine about two weeks ago. I did a search on that person, and they're a dealer in Middle Eastern antiquities."

"You think that's who she got the imp from?"

"With more digging, I could prove it. I feel sure of that."

"Was there a deposit to her account that matched the sum she paid out? Or would have at least covered it?"

"Like money being paid to her by a client? Not before or after. She bought that imp for herself. Not sure why, but that's what it looks like on paper."

I knew why. This new information just confirmed it. "Hang on to this info. Make sure you have copies of everything. I have a feeling we're going to need this very soon."

"You got it."

"Thanks for sharing it with me. I'll talk to you soon."

"You're welcome, Princess." She stopped whispering suddenly and said, "Oh, hi, Hank, what can I—"

The line went dead. I laughed softly, and since I

had work to get done, I put my head down and got to it. I could fill Greyson in on the money news tonight.

By the end of the day I'd gotten most everything accomplished, including running through an inventory of the toy vehicles section with Kip while Juni handled the register. We were surprisingly low on tow trucks. Sure, trucks were always popular, but it was typically the construction stuff that went first.

I said hi to Buttercup and Holly, then rode the elevator up with Juniper and Kip. Kip only had eyes for Juni, which made me want to poke her and point out that I'd been right about him having a crush on her. But that could wait until we disembarked.

She and I got out, he said good-bye and went on up to his floor. As soon as the doors closed, I nudged her. "Told you."

"Told me what?"

"Kip likes you. He gets moony eyes around you. How do you not see that?"

"Because it doesn't exist?" She stuck her tongue out at me, then changed the subject. "What are you doing tonight?"

"Salvatore's with Greyson. I'm in a pizza rut, but it's a delicious one. After dinner, we'll probably go for a little evening stroll." That would cover me being out of the apartment later in case she checked.

She stopped at her door as I stopped at mine. She got her key out. "Have fun. I'm giving myself a pedi and going to bed early with that new Deanna Chase book."

"Kinda jealous." I opened my door. "Hey, we really need a girls' night. And soon."

She nodded as she pushed her door open. "Agreed. Tomorrow night?"

I thought about it. "I think I can swing that."

"Cool. Done. See you tomorrow."

I nodded. "See you tomorrow."

I just hoped it wasn't from the inside of a cell.

Corette called just as I finished giving Spider his dinner. "Hi, how are you?"

"I'm very well, thank you. I hope I'm not interrupting anything."

"Not at all. What's on your mind?"

"I know you've already caught the imp, and this little tidbit of information is probably pointless now, but I wanted to share something new that Pandora just discovered about the creatures."

"Cool, go ahead."

"Apparently, if you breathe on the inside of the box lid, the imp's name should appear. Probably more than once, from what Pandora told me. When bored, they write their names over and over, but without some kind of assistance, the name stays invisible, which is what protects them."

"And breath would do it? Interesting. Not that I'm about to open that box again."

"That's what she read. I suppose we'll never know for sure, but we thought it was fascinating enough to want to share it with you."

"It is." I laughed. "Do you think his name is all over the town, then?"

"I don't know. Based on how much trouble he caused, I don't think he had a chance to be bored in Nocturne Falls."

"You're right about that."

"Well, you enjoy your evening."

"You too, Corette." I hung up and went to change out of my work clothes, the thought of what the imp's name might be lingering. The creature's name was the key to controlling him. Not something I was interested in, but I bet that tidbit would help with Francine.

Which brought my mind back around to the evening's impending activity.

Greyson showed up with the pizza right on time, and as much as I loved Salvatore's, my nerves had taken over. I stared at the hot, gooey pie in front of me...and felt nothing.

I shook my head and looked up at him. "I can't. I mean, I want to, but I have zero appetite."

He closed the box and nodded sympathetically. "It's okay. We can eat later, after this is all over."

"Yeah." But I was bummed. And not myself, which only added to my nerves. I wasn't used to this kind of mixed-up, off-kilter feeling inside me.

His brows lifted. "You need a distraction. We could go for a walk, do some people-watching. Or catch a movie. We could get more ice cream, although if you don't have an appetite for pizza, I suspect you won't have an appetite for that either. What do you feel like doing?"

"Maybe we should go over the camera again. It's hidden right? I thought I didn't want to know where it was because I wouldn't be able to stop looking at it, but now I feel like if you don't show it to me, I won't be able to stop looking for it."

He laughed and pointed to the snap on the pocket of his black leather jacket. "It's right here."

"In the snap? I don't see anything that looks like a camera lens."

"It's just below it. Sticking out of the pocket."

I looked again and saw a small black knot right under the pocket flap. "That's a camera?"

He nodded. "And everything it records will be saved to my phone but also uploaded to a private account in the cloud."

"And your phone is fully charged?"

He gave me a look.

I held my hands up. "Just checking. Very cool."

"Feel better?"

"I don't know. I guess. I really wish we could get this thing over with now."

He slipped his arm around my waist. "I know."

He leaned his forehead against mine. "Do you want to go early? Catch her off guard maybe?"

I pulled away to look at him. "Do you think we could? What if she's not home?"

"She's always home."

"True." I thought about it. "Yes. Let's go now. But you won't have the benefit of darkness to hide in. Is that going to be an issue?"

He shrugged. "Doesn't matter. She's going to see me at some point anyway. And you hold the cards. She either lets us both in or we walk away. *With* the imp. Right?"

My confidence was coming back. "Right. Then we can get her confession on video, turn it in to the Ellinghams and be back here to eat this pizza before it even gets cold. Okay, I know that's an exaggeration, but close."

He smiled. "Let's get everything together and go to the Gresham manor, then."

"All right." I'd already changed into shorts and a tank top after work, and since I wasn't exactly going to have a business meeting with Francine, what I had on was just fine. I did add my leather jacket, though. The toughness of that made me feel better. Then I grabbed one of my cloth Shop-n-Save grocery bags and tucked the imp box into it after checking that the hair ties holding the lid on were secure. They were.

I stuck my feet in my flip-flops, my keys and

phone in my pocket, and hoisted the shopping bag over my shoulder. "I'm ready."

We walked out and rode downstairs, the silence between us contemplative, like we were both going over the possibilities of what might happen tonight. Which we probably were. I know I was.

As we left the warehouse, Greyson took my hand. "It's going to be okay."

I just nodded and answered with a tense smile. Francine was human. That should mean I had nothing to worry about. But supernatural-on-human crime was a huge no-no and a massive wash of anxiety filled me.

He drove, parking a block away. He turned off the engine, then looked at me, throwing his arm over the seat. "It's not like you to be so quiet. Are you that worried?"

I stared through the windshield. "I am. I shouldn't be maybe, but I've got a sense of dread I just can't shake."

"Do you think it's because of the business she's in? Are you worried that she's got some kind of artifact or object that she might use against us?"

I took a breath. "Maybe." I glanced at him. "Do you think that's likely?"

"Everything in her house is packed up. And if she had something that powerful, why wouldn't she have used it when she came to see you in your office?"

"Good point." But the feeling remained even as we got out of the car. "Let's go around back."

"Sure."

We cut through her side yard. The curtains were drawn, and there were a few lights on, but nothing to indicate which room she was in. My pulse picked up and my hands got sweaty. This was crazy. I was a powerful winter elf. She was human. There was nothing for me to be freaked out about.

I tipped my head at Greyson. "Stay on the side, out of sight."

"Yes, ma'am."

I found my determination, marched right up her porch steps, and knocked on the door. He went to the right and stood flat to the wall. Unless Francine came outside, she'd never see him.

It took her a while to answer, and when she finally came to the door, she was wiping her hands on a towel and seemed flustered. "You're early. You said nine. It's not even seven thirty."

"Do you want to do this or not?"

She huffed out a breath before her mouth flattened into a thin, perturbed line. "Yes. Show me the box first."

I pulled it out of the shopping bag. Bringing the imp was dangerous, but without it, there was no way she'd have let me in.

Francine nodded. "Let's get this over with."

"Agreed." I got one foot in. "I brought a friend to keep things fair."

"Fair? What is that—" She recoiled at the sight of Greyson as he appeared behind me. "No. You're not welcome in my house."

"He goes, I go. You've already proven you can't be trusted, so if you don't like my insurance policy, then this deal is off."

She scowled. "I can be trusted."

"Then there shouldn't be an issue with him being here." I was done discussing whether or not Greyson was staying. "Where do you want to do this?"

"Do what?" She held out her hands. "Give me the box and I'll give you the money."

"Yeah, no. We went over that already." I stepped farther inside, enough that Greyson could come in as well.

He did, shutting the door behind him.

I hooked my thumb under the straps of the shopping bag at my shoulder. "I need to see the money. And count it."

She shook her head, but muttered, "Fine." Then she pointed at Greyson. "Don't touch anything while I'm gone. And both of you stay right here."

He held his hands up. "I'm not moving unless I have a reason to."

She humphed and scurried out of the kitchen and up the stairs. Probably going to her bedroom if I had to guess.

I whispered, "Check for the crate."

He nodded and then seemed to disappear and reappear with a whoosh of air. It was just the speed at which he moved, but the effect was all the same. He nodded. "Still in the butler's pantry."

"Good. She must be thinking she's actually going to get to send it now." And having the crate still there meant we had the upper hand when it came to questioning her. She was going to have to explain what that was all about, or she wasn't getting near the imp.

Well, she wasn't getting near the imp regardless, but she didn't know that yet.

Footsteps announced her descent on the steps, and she returned, carrying an envelope. "Here." She thrust it toward me.

"Put it on the table."

She tossed the envelope, but her hand stayed out. "The box."

"First, a question."

She rolled her eyes. "One. That's it. I have a life to get on with."

"I'm sure you do." But I'd ask as many question as it took. "What were you planning to do with the imp?"

Another exasperated sigh. "I already told you,

it's for a client. A client who's as tired of waiting for it as I am."

I'd play along for a second. "What's your client going to do with it?"

"I don't know, I don't care, and I didn't ask." She wriggled her fingers. "Hand it over."

"You're lying. There's no client, is there?"

She paled slightly, then regained her composure and bared her teeth at me. "Give me my property *now*."

"Greyson."

"Right back." He did the disappearing and reappearing thing again, this time returning with the crate in his hands. He set it on the table in front of the money.

I canted my head toward it. "The foam in this shipping crate exactly matches the size and shape of the imp's box. But the mailing address belongs to your husband. I have a pretty good idea what you were planning to do."

She swallowed and took a step back. "I was mailing the imp on behalf of my client. You can't prove anything else."

"Weird that your client would want the imp mailed to your ex-husband, don't you think?" I shrugged, trying to disguise the frustration building inside me. I'd thought this was going to be a lot easier. That she'd gloat about her own cleverness and let slip everything we needed that way. Clearly, I'd been wrong. "If you tell us the truth, I'll tell you the imp's name. Wouldn't that add a nice layer of mischief to whatever it is you want the imp to do?"

Her eyes rounded. That had hit the mark. "I was mailing the imp for my client, who happens to be an old friend of my ex-husband's." She lifted her hand to her throat and clenched her fist as she drew out the words slowly. Like I was an idiot who needed to be spoon-fed.

"I don't believe you. And you're not getting the imp until you tell me your end game. It's that simple."

She smiled. It was a creepy look on her. "You could have had the cash and your life. Now you'll have neither." She yanked her hand away from her throat, flinging something to the ground. The thing, a vial maybe, shattered, and a thin, red vapor wafted up from the shards.

I threw my hand out and built a shield of ice, but the vapor was everywhere. And unlike Greyson, I had to breathe. I could already feel it working on me, whatever it was. "Greyson," I called out, but he was already on it.

He grabbed her and pinned her arms to her sides as he gave her a shake. "What the hell was that?"

"Ancient Egyptian magic," she snarled. "Which will be paralyzing you too, at any moment. I'd rather get rid of you both than have that stupid thing's name anyway."

So that's what was happening to me. I could feel myself growing numb, and my body had begun to ignore my brain's commands to move. I lurched forward with the mobility I had left.

"I don't think so, Francine," Greyson growled. Her wriggling was no match for his strength, but she didn't give up. "I don't need air to survive."

She roared something back at him, but I was more concerned with trying to put the shopping bag down safely before I dropped it and the lid popped off again. Even with the hair ties on it, I didn't want to take a chance.

My legs gave out just as I made it to a kitchen chair. Panic swept through me. Was this the end? All the chocolates I had yet to eat flashed before my eyes. I hoped Greyson and Cooper didn't fight at my funeral. Although, maybe a little fighting would be okay.

I slumped forward, putting the bag down then laying my head on the table. It was all I could do. At this angle, I couldn't see Greyson or Francine, but her snarls and struggling were loud and clear. A few soft thumps reached my ears, too. Maybe she'd hit him?

I wasn't sure. And the light in the room was dimming.

Actually, it was going out altogether.

Snowballs.

When I opened my eyes again, I wasn't immediately sure where I was. I blinked a few times. I was lying down. I sat up, and my head spun as if I was coming off a Saint Nick Slide. "Ugh." I put my hands on my temples.

"Hey, you're awake. You okay?"

I glanced up, happy to hear Greyson's voice. "I guess. What happened? Are we still at Francine's?" I didn't recognize the old plaid couch I was on. Or anything else.

"Yes." He crouched down in front of me. "She used some kind of paralytic on you to immobilize and knock you out. Didn't work on me, obviously, but then she wasn't counting on me being here."

"Good thing you were."

"I'll say. I tried to find the antidote, because she obviously took something to protect herself, but all I came up with was a valise of unlabeled vials in her bedroom, and I wasn't about to try one of those on you without knowing what they were."

"Much appreciated."

He brushed his hand down my cheek, a sudden sadness in his eyes. "I'm not sure what I would have done if that magic had a more drastic effect on you. I think the shield you created saved you from being under longer. Or maybe the stuff she used just doesn't affect elves the way she hoped." He smiled. "What did the ancient Egyptians know about winter elves, anyway?"

"Not much, I'd guess. How long have I been passed out?"

"Not long. About forty-five minutes."

"Long enough." I looked around. Besides the couch, the space was empty except for two metal shelving units against the far wall of exposed cinder block. Up high on that wall, tatty curtains blocked a trio of narrow windows. "Where are we? A basement, right?"

He nodded. "Francine's basement. I figured being down here would help dampen any sound."

Which was when I heard some muffled noises behind me. I turned around. Francine was zip-tied to one of the chairs from the kitchen. And gagged with a kitchen towel. She was glaring at me with the most murderous gaze I'd ever seen.

My brows shot up. Things had just taken a very different direction.

I grabbed Greyson's arm and hauled him upstairs. The basement steps led us back into the kitchen. "What on earth are we supposed to do with her?"

"Interrogate her, just like we planned."

My mouth came open. "Um, I think things have gone a little past that."

He took hold of my shoulders. "Jayne, she tried to kill you. She would have killed both of us."

"But she didn't. And now you have her tied up to a chair with a kitchen towel stuffed in her mouth. Also, I can't believe you brought zip-ties."

He dropped his hands and shrugged. "I had to gag her. She's a screamer. As for the zip-ties, I like to be prepared. A couple of centuries of life experience teaches you a lot."

"Greyson, you seem to be missing what I'm saying. We can't keep her like this forever. At some point, she's going to tell people what we did."

"Not if we stay on plan."

"What plan?" I shook my hands at him. "This isn't part of any plan."

"Lass, you might be freaking out a little."

I took a few breaths and paced. "Yeah, okay, maybe. But we still need to figure out what we're going to do with her."

"We need her to confess, just like we planned from the beginning. If we get her on video saying she planned to take revenge on her husband, then this is over and done with. No one's going to think twice about us restraining her. Especially not after she tried to do you in. Which I also have on video."

"That's probably our only way out of this unscathed now." I stopped pacing. "But she wasn't exactly forthcoming before she used that magic on me. What makes you think she's going to get chatty now?"

"The time tied to a chair may have softened her

up a bit." His gaze took on the glow of his kind. "Or I could give it a try. I was too busy watching over you to question her about anything but an antidote while you were unconscious."

I shook my head. "No, I'll talk to her. Let her know what her options are at this point."

I looked around. The shopping bag with the imp's box was still on the table. I picked it up. "Especially if she gets a reminder of what this is all about."

"You think she's still going to believe you plan on returning the imp to her?"

I looped the handles over my shoulder. "I think she'll believe whatever I can convince her to believe."

"All right. Let's try it."

We marched back into the basement, the slight mustiness filling my nose and making me want to sneeze.

I went straight to Francine and took the towel out of her mouth. She was smart enough not to say anything. "Look, Francine, I'm going to level with you. You screwed up. Big-time. All I wanted was a few questions answered, then you tried to kill me. Do you see how that changed things?"

She nodded meekly. Like she was giving the whole situation serious thought. Maybe Greyson was right. Maybe being bound and gagged had broken her. I turned around and shot him a *how about that?* look.

Then she started to laugh. It was low and throaty at first, then went directly into head-back, full-on maniacal, cuckoo-for-Cocoa-Puffs territory. She finally stopped to catch her breath, shaking her head and grinning. "You're going away for a long time for this. Both of you. You have to know that. Supernatural against human? That's not just frowned upon, that's punished to the full extent of the law."

A chill ran down my spine. We were never going to get her to confess. Not like this anyway. And without a confession, there was really only one way this could end up. With Greyson and me in serious trouble. I'd gotten him into this. I had to get him out.

I shifted my eyes to the shopping bag. I was out of options. Except for one.

I got very close to Greyson and lowered my voice until I was sure only his vampire senses could pick up what I was saying. "Trust me."

His gaze narrowed. "What are you about to do?"

"You'll see. Just go with it. Please. I can handle this."

"Jayne—"

"And make sure you're recording this, because I don't think we're going to get a second shot."

I walked away and picked up the shopping bag, reaching in for the box and pulling it free.

"Jayne."

Uncertainty and concern edged his voice, but I was determined and confident, and nothing was going to stop me at this point. I knew what I was about to do was risky, but I saw no other way. And I wasn't about to let this woman get away with her evil business and harm us in return. She didn't care who she hurt, that much was plain, so we certainly wouldn't be the last.

I held the box in my hands as I approached her. "This imp is very powerful. And very dangerous. I could open this box and tell it to destroy you. Tell it to remove every trace of you from this town."

Fear played in her eyes, and her mouth went slack, erasing her smile. "You wouldn't do that."

"You're right. I wouldn't." I walked to the first narrow window, raised one hand and sealed it shut with a blast of ice. "Because I'm not that kind of woman." I walked to the next two windows and did the same. There could be no way out of the room for the next few minutes. "But you? You were going to do just that to your ex-husband, weren't you?"

Her eyes were wide and focused on the ice I'd just created. "No, I-I would never do that."

"I'm not sure I believe you." I came back to stand in front of her, then lifted my hand toward the door and sealed it with ice as well. I did a quick check of the basement, icing over a few more spots that looked like potential escape routes. With the final crackle of the hard freeze, I faced Francine again. "But I know a way to find out for sure."

I pulled the hair ties off the box and opened it. The imp zipped out, wings buzzing so fast they were a blur of green. He bared his teeth at me and began a stream of high-pitched, unintelligible words that I can only assume were imp curses. The little dude did not look happy.

Then he started flying around the room, looking for a way out, still chattering up an angry storm.

"I have wishes, imp." He glanced at me, marginally interested, but I wasn't sure the words Imari had mentioned were going to be enough. I flipped the lid over, bent my head and breathed on it. His name appeared. At least, I hoped that was his name. I gave it a try. "Hello, Blueberry."

The tirade ceased, and he flew over to me again.

"Hi," he squeaked back.

So far so good. "I'm sorry about trapping you in the box, but you were sort of wrecking my town."

He shrugged. "Sorry."

"I have one wish left, correct?"

He nodded, which moved his entire body up and down.

"Okay, I'm going to make that wish now. It's kind of detailed, so here goes."

Francine strained to get free. "You can't do this."

"Watch me." Speaking of, I glanced at Greyson. "We good?"

He nodded.

I went back to Blueberry. "Tell you what, Blueberry. You give me two more wishes and I'll find you a better place to live than this box, so long as you promise not to pull any more tricks on anyone."

He nodded again, this time making a little trilling noise. He smiled at me, showing off a sharky grin of pointed teeth. Then he held his hand out with two fingers up. "Two," he chirped.

"Excellent. My first wish is that I want you to cast a truth spell over Francine here. This truth spell has to last for…" I thought it over. "How about the rest of her life?"

Greyson snorted.

I looked at him. "You think that's too much?"

Francine hissed out a curse and jerked against the restraints, causing the chair's feet to clatter on the concrete floor. "You can't do this. You're going to ruin me."

Greyson smiled. "I think it's perfect."

I nodded to Blueberry. "Make it permanent. Can you do that?"

He gave me a thumbs-up, then swooped down toward Francine and flew around her head three times. A trail of green sparkles followed him like the tail of a comet. After the third trip, he rejoined me, coming to light on my shoulder.

"Thank you, Blueberry. I'll get to my second wish in a second." Then I faced Francine, smiling grimly. "What were your plans for the imp?"

Her mouth contorted like she was trying to fight the urge to speak. "I…was…going to send it to my ex-husband with a note that the box contained a rare Olmec war amulet."

"I don't know what that is, but obviously it would have guaranteed that he'd open the box, right?" She nodded as I crossed my arms. Out of the corner of my eye, I saw Blueberry cross his too. "And what were you going to have Blueberry do when your ex-husband let him out?"

She grimaced again but finally got the words out. "Kill him. And erase all traces of his existence."

I recoiled. "You're an awful person. Why would you want to kill your ex?"

She groaned. "He ruined my life, took my business away from me and now he's about to publish a book using my research on magical artifacts. I hate him," she screeched. "I hate him and I want him dead." She dropped her head and fell into a fit of weeping.

It was sad, but she would have killed a man. And that was much worse. I backed up until I was next to Greyson. "You get all that?"

He nodded. "Yes."

"Excellent." I turned so I could see Blueberry. "Ready for wish number two?"

He hopped into the air, hovering with excitement. "Ready."

"It's a big one."

He shivered and gave me that pointy grin again. "I can do it."

"Good, because I want you to make right all the

tricks you played on the town. No more Dr Pepper pouring over the falls, no more black wedding dresses, no more fishy smell, nothing. Put it all back to the way you found it."

His little shoulders drooped.

"Blueberry, that's my wish. Then we'll see about your new home. I just need to make a couple calls."

That perked him up a bit. He flew into the center of the room and started spinning. He went faster and faster until there was nothing but a bright, green blur in the air. Then there was a loud pop and a small explosion of green, sparkly dust.

He flew back to me, smiling. "All better."

I nudged Greyson. "Check that out, will you?"

He pulled his phone out. "On it."

"Good. And while you do that, I'll get a hold of someone to take care of Francine."

Didn't take long for the right people to show up, and it didn't surprise me that Cooper was among those who arrived at Francine's.

I greeted him in the yard. "Hey."

"Hey." He glanced at Blueberry, who'd refused to go back in the box and was now napping on my shoulder. "Should I even ask about that or…?"

"Long story short, Blueberry is about to be a free imp."

"Blueberry?"

"Yep."

"Is that why everything in town is back to normal?"

"No, it's because that's what I used my last wish on."

Cooper nodded appreciatively. "Considering all the other things you could have used it for, that was pretty nice of you."

I snorted. "You really think I was going to let all that craziness stand?"

"No, you're not that kind of person."

"That's what I told Francine."

The sheriff and Hugh Ellingham walked up to us. Sheriff Merrow spoke to me first. "We're going to need you to give us a statement, Miss Frost, so don't leave until we're done."

"You got it, Sheriff."

Hugh Ellingham smiled. "I can't wait to hear this one. See you inside."

"We'll be in," Cooper said.

Sheriff Merrow eyed Blueberry. "Going to want to talk to that one too."

"He'll be along with us," I promised.

The Sheriff and Hugh nodded at us and went on to the house.

I watched them until they were inside. Greyson would be showing them the video any minute. I turned back to Cooper. "She would have killed me."

Shock registered on his face. "I'm very glad she didn't."

"Greyson was responsible for that. His being a vampire is what saved us."

Cooper sighed. "Look, he's never going to be the best man when you and I get married, but for his part in keeping you safe, I owe him."

"That's very nice of you to say." I ignored the married comment. "What's going to happen to Francine?"

"I'm not entirely sure. But there'll be some kind of punishment. Especially if her ex-husband wants to press charges. Technically, his ability to read objects makes him a supernatural, and all this business with the imp puts a supernatural bend on things, so most likely, that's the court that will hear this case. Even though she's human."

"It's not like any of this would make sense in a human court anyway."

He shook his head. "No, it wouldn't." Then he exhaled, his expression turning worried. "You didn't call me."

I jerked my thumb toward the house. "I was a little busy."

He frowned. "What I meant is you called Greyson."

"Oh. To do this, you mean."

His frown stayed put.

"Would you have said yes?" I shook my head. "Cooper, I didn't want to put you in a situation that could have caused you trouble. Or made you lose your job. Or made you turn me in."

He stared past me at the house. "I appreciate that. But it makes me feel like you've sided with him. Is that what's happened? Are you about to make a choice?"

"No, I absolutely am not." I leaned in and kissed him, partly to appease him and partly because I needed the reassurance of that intimate contact. Having your life threatened can do that to you. "Can you honestly say I was wrong in my assessment of what your reaction to all this would have been?"

He hesitated. "I wouldn't have turned you in."

"But?"

He rolled his eyes, and a half smile bent his mouth. "I probably would have tried to talk you out of it."

"See?" I poked him in the ribs. "And that's what I love about you. You're a solid, upstanding citizen."

"I'm glad you love something about me." The half-smile turned into a smirk. "That implies Greyson is not, you know."

"Not what?"

"A solid, upstanding citizen."

"Now don't go putting words in my mouth." I tipped my head. "We good?"

"We're good."

"All right. Let's go inside and get the paperwork over with. I still have this imp to take care of."

He laced his fingers with mine as we started walking. He shook his head and laughed softly.

"What?" I asked.

"Nothing. Just you being you."

I was about to say something when a familiar voice called out my name.

We both turned to see Birdie dashing across Francine's lawn.

Cooper snorted. "And just when I thought the night couldn't get any more interesting."

Birdie caught up to us. "Princess Jayne, are you all right? Is Greyson all right? I just heard on the scanner that something was going on over here. Is Francine dead?"

I blinked at her. "No, Francine is not dead. And yes, Greyson and I are both fine."

She suddenly gasped. "Hold still, Princess. The imp is on your shoulder."

Cooper rolled his lips in like he was trying not to laugh.

"I know, Birdie. Blueberry is sleeping. He's had a big night."

Her penciled-in brows scrunched up. "Blueberry?"

I looped my arm through hers. "Walk with us and I'll explain."

As early as possible the next morning, Delaney had Stanhill drive us out to see Matilda Sharpe once again. Rising that early wasn't easy given how late I was up taking care of all the details involved with Francine's nonsense. I'd also called my dad on the globe so he'd know all was well before he read something in the Tombstone, which he now subscribed to. But the early start was important. I wanted to fulfill my promise to Blueberry as soon as I could, lest he think it was all a ruse and get up to mischief again.

Mattie had graciously offered to give Blueberry a home, and he seemed thrilled to be offered the job of guardian of the bees. Especially since he was so fond of their honey.

The handover went smoothly, and when we got back to the warehouse, I invited Delaney up before

I got out of the car. "Come on. I want to introduce you to someone."

She gave me a curious look. "What have you got up your sleeve?"

"Nothing, I swear. But I wouldn't ask if it wasn't important."

She leaned forward to speak to Stanhill. "I'll be right back."

We got out and rode the elevator up. Spider greeted us with a full front shot of his belly on display from the couch. "Don't mind my cat. I haven't taught him to wear pants yet."

Delaney went right over and gave him some tummy rubs, which secured her place as Spider's new best friend, I'm sure. "Oh, he's such a sweet baby! And so little. My cat Captain is a beast. Stanhill sneaks him bacon every chance he gets."

"Spider doesn't seem that interested in people food. Fortunately." I picked up the globe from the side table and gave it a shake.

Didn't take long for my dad to answer. "Hi, sweetheart. All set?"

"Hi, Dad. All set."

He gave me a wink, then disappeared off-globe.

Delaney came and stood at my side, most likely curious about what I was up to. It wasn't every day you saw someone using a snow globe as a communication device.

My aunt appeared in the glass. "Hello, darling."

She waved at me. "Is that your little vampire friend?"

I laughed. "Yes, Aunt Martha. This is Delaney Ellingham." I turned to Delaney. "This is my aunt Martha, maker of the fudge you like so much."

Delaney let out a soft squeal. "That fudge is genius. You're a genius. It's the best thing ever. Did Jayne tell you that I'm just dying to sell it in my shop?"

Aunt Martha beamed with pride. "She did. And I wanted to let you know that I'm willing to work something out with you. I can't give you the recipe, of course, but I think a few batches of fudge a week would be doable."

More squealing. Then Delaney hugged me. "You're awesome." She grinned at my aunt. "You're even awesomer. Thank you so much."

"You're very welcome, dear. And congratulations on your little one."

Delaney put her hand on her belly. "Thank you. I'm due the end of October, so my staff will be handling things at the shop for a few months after that, but I assure you the fudge will be in good hands."

My aunt nodded. "Jayne has told me all about you and your shop. I have no worries."

"Aunt Martha, I'll call you back later tonight and we can work out the details, okay?"

"Very good, Jaynie. I'll talk to you later, then."

She glanced at someone off screen. "How do you turn this thing off?"

She disappeared and the snow stopped swirling. I put the globe back in its spot. "There you go. I'll call you tomorrow and tell you how she wants to proceed."

"Anything is fine with me. I just want that fudge in my store for Christmas." She shook her head. "Thank you again. This makes my day."

"You're welcome. You hooked me up with Mattie, and her honey is what made capturing the imp possible, so..." I shrugged. "I just wanted to find a way to say thanks."

"Well, you did it." She checked her watch. "I better run. I need to get a couple batches of cookies done before the shop opens."

"I definitely don't want to stand in the way of baking." I saw Delaney out, then took a long, hot shower in an attempt to wake myself up a little more. I was going to be a little late to work, but frankly, today I didn't care. I deserved a late morning after the last couple of days.

And things still weren't entirely figured out. My supply of Dr Pepper hadn't stopped magically replenishing itself, but Spider hadn't said a word since I'd returned home last night. I had no idea if his ability to talk had been one of the things Blueberry had fixed or not.

I got ready for work, drying my hair and fixing

my makeup. I contemplated the finished product in the mirror. Thankfully, the ancient magic Francine had used on me didn't seem to have any lasting effects.

In the living room, Spider was still asleep on the couch. I gave him a little scratch on the head. "Are you going to sleep all day?"

He yawned and stared sleepily up at me. "Spider tired."

"I guess that answers that." So the Dr Pepper and Spider's voice were permanent. Maybe because they'd been wishes? Accidental wishes, but wishes all the same. Interesting. "See you after work, baby."

I grabbed my purse and went down to my office. I tossed my purse on my desk, then headed into the shop. Juniper and Kip had things well in hand.

I slid behind the counter to hang with Juni for a few minutes. "Did you hear about last night?"

She nodded. "Word spreads fast in this town."

"Yes, it does."

"Doesn't mean I don't want to know all the details." Then she peered at me, and concern marred her pretty face. "You okay?"

"Yep. A little tired."

"But not injured or anything?"

"Nope. Although…I could be better."

"Oh?"

I nodded. "I could use a girls' night in. You, me and Buttercup. What do you say?"

She grinned. "I say you're on."

"Perfect. I'll bring the pizza. And some ice cream."

"I thought you just had pizza last night?"

I sighed and shook my head. "Never got around to it with all the excitement."

She snorted softly. "Tonight's going to seem pretty boring after that."

I smiled, utterly happy with the thought of doing nothing but hanging out with my friends and not worrying one bit about who might be plotting to revenge. Or worse.

"Good. Boring is *exactly* what I want."

Want to be up to date on all books & release dates by Kristen Painter? Sign-up for my newsletter on my website, www.kristenpainter.com. No spam, just news (sales, freebies, and releases.)

If you loved the book and want to help the series grow, tell a friend about the book and take time to leave a review!

Other Books by Kristen Painter

COZY MYSTERY:

Jayne Frost series
Miss Frost Solves A Cold Case: A Nocturne Falls Mystery

PARANORMAL ROMANCE

Nocturne Falls series
The Vampire's Mail Order Bride
The Werewolf Meets His Match
The Gargoyle Gets His Girl
The Professor Woos The Witch
The Witch's Halloween Hero – short story
The Werewolf's Christmas Wish – short story
The Vampire's Fake Fiancée
The Vampire's Valentine Surprise – short story
The Shifter Romances The Writer
The Vampire's True Love Trials – short story

Sin City Collectors series
Queen of Hearts
Dead Man's Hand
Double or Nothing
Box Set

STAND-ALONE PARANORMAL ROMANCE

Dark Kiss of the Reaper

Heart of Fire

Recipe for Magic

Miss Bramble and the Leviathan

URBAN FANTASY

The House of Comarré series:

Forbidden Blood

Blood Rights

Flesh and Blood

Bad Blood

Out For Blood

Last Blood

Crescent City series:

House of the Rising Sun

City of Eternal Night

Garden of Dreams and Desires

Nothing is completed without an amazing team.

Many thanks to:

Cover design: Keri Knudson
Interior formatting: Author E.M.S
Editor: Joyce Lamb
Copyedits/proofs: Marlene Engel

About the Author

Kristen Painter is a little obsessed with cats, books, chocolate, and shoes. It's a healthy mix. She loves to entertain her readers with interesting twists and unforgettable characters. She currently writes the best-selling paranormal romance series, Nocturne Falls, and award-winning urban fantasy. The former college English teacher can often be found all over social media where she loves to interact with readers. Visit her web site to learn more.

www.kristenpainter.com